TRAIL OF THE FAST GUN

Beautiful Elena Barker secures Ben Darringer's release from prison. Her bargain: a pardon for killing her brother — if he can save her father's ranch from ruthless encroachers. As a hired gun in the midst of an all-out range war, Ben is forced to take justice into his own hands. The greedy cattlemen have recruited the sinister gunslinger Zevala, and a confrontation is unavoidable. But does Ben stand a chance against the fastest gun in the territory?

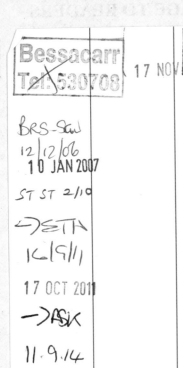

LEE MARTIN

TRAIL OF THE FAST GUN

Complete and Unabridged

LINFORD
Leicester

First published in the
United States of America

First Linford Edition
published 1999

British Library CIP Data

Martin, Lee, *1943* –
Trail of the fast gun.—Large print ed.—
Linford western library
1. Western stories
2. Large type books
I. Title
813.5'4 [F]

ISBN 0–7089–5552–5

Published by
F. A. Thorpe (Publishing) Ltd.
Anstey, Leicestershire

Set by Words & Graphics Ltd.
Anstey, Leicestershire
Printed and bound in Great Britain by
T. J. International Ltd., Padstow, Cornwall

This book is printed on acid-free paper

To my sister Arlene, with whom I share many exciting and wonderful memories, and who has been an inspiration with her wit and joyous approach to life on her primitive mountain.

1

Yuma Prison was no place for a lady, but there she stood in blue velvet and a dark veil, smelling of sweet roses. At her side was the grisly old guard known as Toothless.

The corroded bars between Ben Darringer and his visitor reminded him that he was a gunfighter with a life sentence for murder. On his side of the barrier were the stench of the filthy cell and the memory of an old man who had died in his arms the night before.

Alone in the nine-by-eight cell, he had been dreaming of Caroline and expecting his brother Jess, not this mysterious woman.

Her voice, as soft as the hush of dawn, had just set forth something incredible.

'You heard her,' Toothless grunted.

'You got a chance to get out o' here. All you gotta do is work for her.'

'Can I see that paper you're talking about?' Ben asked.

A small, slender, white-gloved hand passed the rolled and ribboned paper through the bars. As he took it, her fingers recoiled as if in fear of touching him.

Conscious of his bedraggled appearance, his beard and sweat, Ben also drew away. Unrolling the paper, he saw the signature and seal of the territorial governor. His gaze slowly found the pertinent paragraphs:

And as Miss Elena Barker has sworn that she was an inadvertent witness to what was actually a fair fight between her brother, Rex Barker, and the gunfighter, Ben Darringer, but was heretofore afraid to come forward, it appears that there is a reasonable doubt as to the charge of homicide and the resulting conviction. Had Miss Barker testified at the Tucson trial in March of 1876, there is reason to believe that the verdict might have been one of not guilty.

Ben's throat was dry, his grip damp on the heavy paper. Certain that there had been no witnesses, yet driven by the pain in his gut, he read on:

Whereas Miss Barker has offered to employ him and be responsible for his behavior, I have recommended and been assured of his parole for one year. During this period, there shall be no restriction on his use of firearms in order to protect Miss Barker and her family. I would be inclined at the end of that one-year period, based on her report, to grant him a full pardon.

Ben Darringer had studied law and was no man's fool. It was a convoluted plot allowing her to hire his gun. 'Well?' Toothless grunted.

3

'What did you tell the governor?' Ben asked her.

'That what you said at the trial was true. My brother's gun was in his hand. He was going to kill you, but you suddenly drew so fast that you fired before he could.'

Her voice wavered with the weight of her words, but she spoke the truth, whether or not she realized it.

'You want outa here?' Toothless demanded.

'I'm considerin',' Ben said.

He knew his answer would be yes. He had already spent a year in Arizona's territorial prison. All those nights with one blanket and a skimpy straw tick for a mattress had not been lost on him. So far, he had escaped tuberculosis, but time would take its toll.

Last night that poor old soul had died in his arms. Ben could still see his pale eyes and feel the trembling fingers on his shirt. Ben had cried.

Now he was alone, but there were six bunks, often making it so crowded that the stench was unbearable. There was no privacy. Midsummer heat, due again in weeks, would be stifling.

'Hey, Darringer, what you gonna do?' the guard demanded.

Slowly, Ben rolled up the paper and handed it back.

'This on record?' he asked.

'Yes,' she said. 'It takes effect the moment you agree.'

'And what kind of work are you expecting?'

'You'll herd cattle at our ranch in Thunder Valley.'

'I heard there was trouble up there.'

Toothless wiped his mouth, impatient. 'Well?'

'I'll work for you, Miss Barker,' Ben said.

Relief and wonder were welling up within him, but that pain was still in his gut. How many men would he have to kill before the pardon was granted? That land was open range, and the fight had to be over grass or water. He'd been through that before.

5

It was no picnic. But neither was Yuma Prison.

'I'll be back this afternoon,' she said. 'I'll ask the superintendent to see that you have a bath.'

Toothless grunted, then led her away.

The scent of roses lingered. Ben's throat was so dry that it hurt. He wasn't sure if he could stand one more hour in this rat hole. She made him think of Caroline, sweet, lovely Caroline, who had rejected him the moment he was arrested.

He sat down on his bunk, his face in his hands as if that would make it all go away. There was a stench all around. Trembling, he whispered a prayer of thanks.

At the rattle of chains, he looked up. In the corridor, guards were marching a drooping, delirious man back from the dungeon, known as the Snake Den. Sooner or later, it would have been his turn in there with an occasional slithery visitor.

When he was finally in the big tub of hot water in the hospital area, scrubbing himself with glee, his brother Jess arrived, as expected. As tall as but leaner than Ben, with lots of tussled brown hair and needing a shave, Jess sat on the nearby bench. He had Ben's gray eyes, only darker.

The squat guard at the door, half asleep, ignored them and walked off in the hallway, out of earshot.

Jess was full of talk. Only twenty-seven and five years younger than Ben, he saw wonder in everything, had the purest heart, and was gifted with a clear singing voice and a talent for the guitar.

'Hey, Ben, what are you doin' in here? You got lice? Listen, you can't believe what I just seen out there.'

'Well, you won't believe — '

'I mean, there they are, big as life, buildin' a bridge across the Colorado between here and California. A railroad bridge, can you believe it?'

'Jess, I have to tell you something.'

7

'I mean, pretty soon a man won't have a night on the prairie without some tootin' iron horse goin' by. What with steamboats goin' up the Colorado and railroads crisscrossin', a man's gonna have trouble bein' by himself.'

'Jess, I'm getting out of here.'

Jess paused, suddenly dumbfounded, and then he listened to Ben's story with astonishment. Ben lay back in the tub as Jess obliged and poured more hot, clean water on him.

'All I have to do is work for her,' Ben said.

'Yeah, sure. Well, I've heard the Barkers got most of the valley and are tryin' to keep others out. I'm gonna be comin' up there with a Texas herd — fella by the name of Shockley. He's on his way up the Goodnight-Loving Trail and across. I'll be meetin' him somewhere around Camp Bowie.'

'Is he hirin' your rope or your gun?' Ben asked.

'Well, I reckon the name Darringer means a fast gun.'

'That isn't your line of work, Jess.'

'Nope, but I figured I could ride on your reputation till I get me a stake. You're as well known as Wes Hardin and Jesse James, and I'll bet you could even take Zevala.'

Ben shrugged. He wasn't sure he liked being mentioned in the same breath as Zevala, the Texas killer.

'I heard,' Jess said, 'that some fella did a survey right through the valley afore the War Between the States. With the railroad comin' and the Apaches gone to the reservation, that's mighty attractive land.'

'Sounds like a fight, all right.'

'You know, Ben, if Clay and Hank hadn't taken on them carpetbaggers back in '74, you wouldn't be in this mess.'

'They were framed,' Ben said. 'They were protecting that widow, but no one bothered to have her testify. I didn't hear about it till they were about to be hanged.'

'Well, the Darringers always have to

get in the middle of things. We can't ever be neutral. So you busted 'em out, but nobody knew you done it. I'm right sorry you didn't go back to studyin' law after that.'

'Didn't seem right,' Ben said.

'So you got mixed up in range wars. Then you finally came to Tucson to join up with me. And that's where you met Caroline.'

With a shrug, Ben remembered the romance. He would have gone back to Texas for her, finished his law, gained the approval of her family. Except that the Barkers' son had crossed his trail.

Ben sank down into the hot water, sad about the past but grateful that he was getting a second chance. He soaked peacefully, listening as Jess rambled on. Jess was the big talker in the family.

'The Darringers ain't amounted to much, have they? Clay, he's twenty-nine about now, and Hank is a year older, and they're both on the run. You are here and I'm as restless as a hungry coyote. I tell you, Ben, the

Darringers are a sorry bunch. But if you get that pardon, maybe it'll be good luck for us.'

Ben slid deep into the water as he answered:

'It would please me mighty fine. I'd finish my law study with that judge. Then I'd work on a pardon for Clay and Hank.'

Reluctantly, Ben stood up, and grabbing the big soiled towel, he tried to dry himself off. Jess continued his gab.

'I've been thinkin'. Maybe this winter I'll head back down to Texas and see Ma.'

'I've been thinking about her a lot,' Ben said.

They were silent a minute, thinking of their mother, who became a widow when their father was killed by bandits six months before Jess, the youngest, was born. She had remarried within a year and raised a new brood. The four older brothers had left as soon as they were able.

11

Jess leaned back, folding his arms as he continued:

'It's a shame, your not gettin' a chance to hang up your shingle and marry Caroline Frost. Now I hear she's going to — ' Jess broke off, and he looked sorry about his words.

'Going to what?' Ben asked.

'Marry Rich Shockley, that's what. You'll be seein' her, I reckon. But maybe you don't care, seeing as how she ran out on you.'

Ben felt pain in his middle, and he couldn't answer.

Toothless appeared with a clean, double-breasted shirt that just fit Ben's large chest and shoulders. Ben was tall, and lean from the waist down. The new, deep blue Levi's were stiff and harsh. His old boots and black hat were added.

Though clean-shaven, he felt the roughness of his square face and jaw. Sweat was on the slight hook of his nose. He smoothed his collar-length black hair. His cool gray eyes narrowed as he felt for his missing holsters.

'All right,' Toothless said. 'Let's go, the both of you.'

In the superintendent's office, the veiled woman was sitting near the desk, hands neatly clasped in her lap. She sat erect, still scented with roses. Beside her stood an old, crusty cowhand, arms folded, his wrinkled face grim. His handle-bar mustache was gray-red. His rusty hair was receding and his hat was thrown back from the chin strap.

On the desk lay Ben's gun belt with the prized Colts still in the cut-down holsters. His old, fringed leather jacket was folded beside them.

'Well, Darringer,' said the bearded superintendent who was known as Old Grubby, 'I see by the record you're an educated man. I don't know what twist of fate turned you from law to bein' a gunfighter, but now you have a chance to start a new life. I don't want you back here.'

'I'll make it a point,' Ben said.

'Sign here for your belongings.'

Ben gladly bent over the desk and signed his name. He stared at it. *Benjamin Darringer*. Dreams shattered. No shingle with his name on it. No Caroline. A shaky future.

Slowly, carefully, he picked up the heavy gun belt, strapping it on so that it hung low on his hips. He resisted resting his hands on the Colts. The weight felt good.

'Mr. Darringer,' the woman said, 'I would like you to meet Wash Gridley, our foreman. We'll be taking the steamer upriver, then across by wagon. At Crescent Ranch we'll be picking up a herd of horses.'

The meeting was concluded, and Ben picked up his long jacket. The woman left first, walking with the superintendent. Jess and Ben followed Gridley.

Outside the front gate, the superintendent walked Miss Barker to the wagon with its team of bays. Gridley followed them.

Ben drew a deep breath of warm,

free air. He turned to Jess and grinned, and they threw their arms around each other in a good, solid hug. Then they drew back and shook hands.

'I gotta head east to pick up Shockley's herd,' Jess said. 'Will you go along with this, or are you goin' to try a getaway?'

Ben considered his brother's question for a moment, then shrugged. His voice was low, his eyes on Gridley: 'I'll take my chances with the Barkers.'

'Well, I've never trusted any woman,' Jess told him. 'So you be mighty careful. She could turn on you, just as soon as she gets what she wants.'

They shook hands again. Jess pulled on his hat and walked over to his buckskin. Ben watched as Jess mounted and strapped on his six-gun. They said a last good-bye and Jess rode away.

Ben felt a sudden emptiness, a need for family, for roots, for a fireplace with his three brothers gathered around, as when they were children. He recalled his mother's rocking and sewing.

'Remember, Ben,' she had said on his departure, 'there's a lot of injustice in this world. I like to think you'll be out there fixin' it and not givin' it.'

When he'd gotten the chance to study law with a crusty old judge, he had written to her, knowing it would please her. Then his life had fallen apart. But despite two years of being in trouble, he had tried to return to the study of law. That had impressed Caroline and her position-conscious family. And then Rex Barker attacked him. It seemed a century ago.

Turning, Ben saw the wagon waiting, with the woman sitting erect and away from the big man who was holding the reins. Two drooping bay horses were in harness.

Gridley came over to him. The man was of average height but strong of build. His hands were big and mean, and his face had years of courage and fight driven deep in its crinkles. His mustache jerked as he talked.

'All right, Darringer, I reckon you

16

know we'll be going into Yavapai and Apache country.'

Ben nodded. The Apaches had been driven to the San Carlos reservation in 1875, just after Cochise died, but there were some renegades who had broken out and were raiding along the border and to the north. He'd heard that one group was making its way toward Prescott and raiding isolated ranches.

'Worse than that,' Gridley said, 'there's no tellin' who might be lookin' to ambush us. Every small rancher in the valley is fightin' us over grass. I just hope you're as good with them guns as the lady thinks you are.'

Ben started to answer, but shrugged instead. His reputation was getting him out of prison. He wasn't going to argue.

He drew deep breaths of free air as he followed Gridley to the wagon. As they climbed into the creaking bed, he caught the scent of roses and began to wonder who was under the veil. But it didn't matter. This woman could turn

17

on him as soon as her trouble ended. In fact, he would bet on it.

But Ben was ready to fight for his freedom. As the wagon lurched toward the river, he took a last, long look at the rambling prison, swearing he would never return.

2

The stern-wheeler had two noisy engines turning the great red wheel. Ben figured it was about a hundred and thirty feet long and forty feet wide. It had two decks and passenger cabins up front on the upper deck. The pilot-house was tall and ungainly, and it hovered over the cabin area. Forward was the tall, black chimney, trailing smoke.

On the lower deck, the wagon and team were crowded in with cattle and horses and other vehicles. A shaggy dog was making a nuisance of itself, running between the legs of animals and barking. An old man was yelling at it.

On the upper deck, the air was fresher. Only the front half of the deck was covered, and Ben walked through the crowd in the open space. From the railing, he could see rocky red banks and vast prairie spreading to the horizons. He longed to be in the saddle out there, alone.

Black smoke alternately puffed and trailed in the sky above. The engine chugged and snorted. Sometimes the craft seemed uncertain which way it was going. The river was wide and often choppy. The boat often rocked and always vibrated.

Among the passengers were soldiers and settlers with children. Some would be headed for Fort Mojave. Possessions were piled everywhere, covered with canvas.

Gridley came over to his side. The wind blew at their faces as they gazed upriver.

'Sure is a strange place for cowhands,' Gridley said.

'Do we have to spend a night on this thing?'

'Yep, but it ain't so bad. Kinda rocks you like you were in the cradle. But I'm sure ready to get back to the ranch.'

'Big, is it?'

'As big as a man can hold. Miss Barker there, her mother's family had some kind of Spanish land grant, but the government is takin' its time on it. Meanwhile, we got farmers and small ranchers crowdin' us.'

'And Shockley.'

'I hear he's comin', all right. He's already got a ranch set up at the east end of the valley, near the fort. From what I hear, he's sure to bring in a lot of hired guns. And us near to roundup.'

'What size herd have we got?'

'Twenty thousand right now. Need every bit of grass. Just got one of them white-faced bulls. It's so short and fat that I got my doubts about its knowin' what to do with a longhorn cow.'

Gridley pointed toward the eastern bank, where something fuzzy and white was moving like a herd of tumbleweeds over the red earth.

'Looky there,' he said. 'Sheep. Why, they're all over now. Some big ranch over at Flagstaff is the worst. Hear they got fifty thousand head or more. Country ain't the same.'

'So what can you do about it?' Ben asked.

'I'm thinkin' of Oregon. I mean, after things settle down for the Barkers.'

'How long have you been with them?'

'Five years.'

Ben recognized loyalty in a man, and he respected it. He knew he was going to like this tough cowhand, maybe more than might be prudent. Trust could come too soon.

Ben stiffened as the Barker woman appeared in the crowd. She walked toward them unveiled, and he was stunned by what he saw. Her long black hair was glistening in the sunlight, blowing in the wind, away from a warm, splendid face. Her lips were delicately carved and her cheek-bones were high. Her soft throat was exposed above her lace collar. She wore a blue velvet jacket over a flowing blue skirt. She was beautiful. Breathtaking. He hadn't expected that.

'Close your mouth,' Gridley said with a laugh.

Ben watched her as she paused by a large family. She talked to the heavy woman who was holding a crying baby. Soon the baby was in Elena Barker's arms.

The little one stopped crying and gripped Elena's long, flowing hair. How natural she looked as she rocked the baby and spoke to it. Elena's smile was gentle and loving.

Ben watched, fascinated. Then Elena returned the child and walked over to him and Gridley. They both tipped their hats. Ben couldn't help staring at her. Her dark blue eyes were glistening under long lashes. He looked for hostility in her but saw none.

'Mr. Darringer,' she said in that hushed voice, 'it doesn't appear that you're seasick.'

'Reckon not,' he said.

She put smooth, pale hands on the

railing and gazed toward the eastern bank. Her peach-colored face was damp from the heat.

'Sheep,' she said.

'Yes, ma'am,' Gridley responded.

As she stood by the rail, the wind in her hair, she reminded Ben of a painting he had once seen in a museum. He remembered it well: It was of a woman waiting on shore for her whaler husband's return; she gazed into infinity.

'Everything's changing,' she said. 'Before long, Arizona will be a state. Railroads will bring the farmers.'

'Too many people comin' here,' Gridley agreed. 'Afore you know it, they'll be buildin' new towns. They'll be playin' that there baseball in Tucson.'

'Everyone will know where they stand,' she said. 'There'll be fences, limits, new laws.'

'Well, we sure ain't got that in Thunder Valley,' Gridley said.

After a few moments of silence she retired to her cabin.

'She's got breeding,' Gridley said. 'Her ma's bound and determined that Elena's gonna marry well. That ain't you by a darn sight.'

Ben had to grin and shake his head.

On deck that night, Gridley furnished him with beef jerky and cold biscuits. They slept in blankets on the hard wooden deck, along with most of the other passengers. Only a few had enough money for the cabins.

The ship went slower at night, rocking gently. The roar of the engines seemed far away.

For the first time in a year, Ben slept a peaceful sleep, his Colts inside his blanket. He was ready to get back on land, eager to be back in the saddle. He yearned for the creak of leather and the sweat of a good horse.

In the morning, where the riverbanks were low and the water shallow, the steamer maneuvered within fifty feet of land. The gangway, stretching some twenty feet across, was lowered into the water.

With the help of crewmen and two soldiers, Ben and Gridley lowered the heavy wagon into the water behind the team. It wasn't easy. Elena was on the wagon seat, reins taut in her hands.

They floated the outfit until the horses found the soft sand, dug their hooves in, and pulled it up to the solid ground. The steamer backed away and continued upstream.

Ben relaxed in the rear of the wagon. Lazily, he stretched out while Gridley sat erect, slapping the reins on the rumps of the bays.

Elena Barker sat straight on the wagon seat, never looking back. She was wearing a wide-brimmed hat, tied under her chin with a blue ribbon. She had to be terribly hot in the blue velvet she was wearing.

The steamer was disappearing, leaving its trail of black smoke behind the red ridges. It seemed out of place in this wild land.

The country they crossed was prairie, set with sage and scattered cacti. Red earth sprang forth here and there. Crimson bluffs appeared from time to time. Spotted antelope sprang out of a wash in midafternoon. They scattered with their white tails bobbing. Ben was delighted by the beautiful animals. He swallowed the clean air and freedom with pleasure.

On the road, they met a half dozen soldiers from Camp Mojave. The men were patrolling the road between the fort and Prescott, which ran mostly west to east. The wagon was headed northeast, crossing it.

'Yavapai,' a crusty sergeant told them. 'As tough as any Apache. So watch yourselves.'

'We'll be at the Crescent Ranch by tomorrow night,' Gridley told them.

'You be careful, ma'am,' the sergeant added. 'Right sorry I can't ride along with you, but we got orders to keep on the road.'

Elena smiled at the man as the wagon moved onward. It continued without further stops. By evening they were out of the open land and into a rise of foothills set with crimson bluffs and deep, washed-out gullies. Brush was scattered among the stunted junipers.

They made camp with a small fire hidden deep in a circle of high rocks. Gridley gave Ben a Winchester repeater. Ben kept it at his side as he watched Gridley stir the beans over the fire. He wondered why the woman wasn't cooking. She was sitting off by herself, watching. *Pampered*, Ben thought.

Gridley took her a tin plate of beans. She ate in silence, listening to the men.

'Ever fought any Apache?' the fore-man asked Ben.

'Comanches, mostly.'

'I hear tell the Comanches fight mostly on horseback. Apache and Yavapai, they ain't got no pattern you can figure. One day you'll be ridin' along and they'll spring up out o' the dirt where they was covered up. Mostly, you never see or hear 'em till it's too late.'

Gridley took up his rifle and went out to stand guard.

Elena Barker turned into her blankets under the wagon. Ben sat watching her, thinking of Caroline. He had trouble sleeping and, toward early morning, was easily awakened by the old cowhand.

'Watch yourself,' Gridley said. 'I smell trouble.'

From his perch in the distant rocks, Ben could see Elena's slight form tossing. The moon was bright. The land was silent. Not even a coyote howling. No rustle of the night owl. Nothing. His skin began to crawl.

He stood up and looked around. The sage wasn't moving — or was it? He tightened his grip on the Winchester, a shell already in the chamber. Sweat formed on his face. The hair on his neck was rising.

Suddenly, a huge arm slapped around his throat from behind. As he pulled the trigger on the Winchester, the explosion shattered the stillness. He saw the knife coming down on his chest. He grabbed both arms of his attacker, the Winchester rattling into the rocks.

They rolled in the dust, fighting for the knife. He heard Elena scream. Then he heard gunfire.

His assailant's face was hideous with hate. Yavapai. Grunting for breath, Ben twisted the man's hard wrist until the knife jerked free. With a fierce yell, the attacker tried to pull out Ben's guns, but Ben slammed his fist in the man's face. They wildly gripped each other's wrists.

The near-naked Indian smelled of bear grease and was slippery. He was powerful, like a railroad engine, and unrelenting. Ben fought with all his might, his lungs crying for breath.

Again they rolled together in the dust. Suddenly, Ben took a chance as they struggled to their knees. He freed his right hand and reached for a Colt while the Indian grabbed for the fallen knife.

As the blade came up again, Ben

pulled the trigger in the man's chest. It went off with a loud blast.

The shot echoed in the night. In the flash of light he saw the blazing black eyes. The knife slid down Ben's arm and into his shirt. The attacker gasped, fighting for the knife to his last breath. He crumpled his heavy weight against Ben, who shoved him aside.

The Yavapai, with blood on his bare chest, rolled over into the red sand. Even in death, hatred showed in his glazed eyes. He was a still mound of fury. Ben wiped his face with the back of his hand. He tried to catch his breath while his heart hammered in his chest.

Suddenly, he was aware of fighting and struggling at the camp on the other side of the rocks. Colt in hand, he jumped over the barrier and ran toward Gridley, who was fighting hand to hand with another Yavapai. Ben fired as he ran, and the Indian fell backward with a yell.

Beyond the wagon, horses snorted

as two other attackers tried to pull Elena upon one of their horses. She was fighting furiously, but one had her long hair wound around his fist. She kicked and squirmed and clawed at them. She screamed.

As Ben ran toward them, the bigger of the Indians slammed his fist against her jaw and she collapsed. The other Indian let go of her hair as he saw Ben charging. He drew up an old Springfield and tried to pull the trigger.

Ben's bullet struck the man in the face and he spun backward. The second Indian leaped at Ben with the biggest knife he had ever seen.

Ben jumped aside and fired again. With shock on his face, the Indian fell backward, clawing at his neck where the blood spurted.

Though dead and sprawled on the ground, the two attackers looked as fierce as if they were alive. Short and powerful, giants of the prairie, they lay still in the first light of dawn.

Ben drew a deep breath and rushed

toward Elena. She lay in a heap, unconscious.

She appeared so delicate in form and face that he was afraid to touch her, but he knelt at her side. The Indian ponies snorted and ran away. Ben hesitated, still trying to catch his breath as he holstered his Colt.

'Well, pick her up,' Gridley said from behind him. 'I'll keep an eye out, but I figure that's all of 'em.'

Ben didn't know how to do it. Oh, he had courted Caroline, but that had all been proper and hands off. This was something new to him. Elena Barker was beautiful, aristocratic, unapproachable.

He turned and looked up at Gridley, but the man was holding his left arm in pain, with blood on his fingers.

Ben felt around in the dimming moonlight, his right arm sliding around her legs. It made him tremble. His left arm slid behind her waist. Clumsily, he lifted her. She was small, but heavier than he had expected.

Her head rolled against his shoulder as he crooked his elbow behind her back. She was wearing her day clothes, but her jacket was open, and the lace-trimmed bodice was ripped at the collar. Her throat was white, smooth, delicate.

'Get her over to the fire,' Gridley said.

As he carried her, Ben smelled the roses from her soft skin. At the side of the tiny fire, he slowly lowered her. He liked her silky black hair against his chest and trailing down his arm. As she lay supine, he watched Gridley place a blanket under her head.

Ben drew back and sat on his heels. Gridley took precious water from his canteen, wet his bandanna and pressed it to her brow.

'He hit her pretty hard,' Ben said.

'She'll be all right. Women just wear all them tight clothes. Here, bind me up, will you?'

Ben tore the man's shirt, baring the slice in the tough flesh. It was a clean wound, and Ben washed it off and bound it with another bandanna from the cowhand's bedroll.

'I'll scout around,' Ben said. 'Be morning soon.'

He recovered the Winchester and searched the area carefully. There was no sign of more Yavapai, but any bush could suddenly move and spring to life. He waited until full dawn before he returned to camp. The red sky in the east was a warning, he thought.

Gridley had dragged the bodies out of sight into a nearby wash. Elena was sitting by the fire with a mug of coffee. Her lace front had been refastened.

She looked up as Ben approached. He knew she was still frightened. It was in her blue eyes and tight lips.

'Are you all right?' he asked.

'Yes, thank you,' she responded.

She was staring at Ben. He felt uncomfortable and tried to concentrate on his coffee. Then Gridley spoke.

'We've been talkin' about you. I ain't never seen a white man could fight on the run like that. You never missed a shot, and it was hardly light.'

Ben shrugged. The old man was praising him, and he appreciated it, but he longed for the day when a man would shake his hand for some other reason.

He looked at Elena, but she was avoiding his gaze now.

After breakfast they hitched up the wagon. The horses were still nervous, snorting and pawing the red earth. There was no sign of the ponies. Ben climbed into the back with his Winchester and reloaded Colts. There would be no relaxation now.

All day they traveled, stopping only to rest and water the horses. The land was rugged, rising often into high brushy chunks of bluff. Sometimes the earth was bright red, and sometimes it was white and dusty. The air was always hot and thin. By evening, they sighted the Crescent Ranch.

Settled in a round, high-walled canyon, the house and sheds were

36

adobe with some timber used to patch and prop. It was dusty, dry, and unfriendly. In the rear of the box canyon, there were corrals stocked with about twenty nervous mustangs, hardheaded and full of grit.

In a side corral, three handsome horses stood at attention. Two were sorrels and one was a big muscled bay, a mountain horse.

As they approached in the wagon, a bent old man with a rifle emerged from the house. He was all whiskers and dirt and wore suspenders over his red flannel underwear. He squinted at them, then waved.

'That's Pa Holder,' Gridley said through his teeth. 'He'd as soon shoot ya as look at ya, but he's one heck of a mustanger. Them other horses belong to us.'

Two other men appeared, equally whiskered and dirty.

'Sid and Saul,' Gridley said. 'Holder's sons. They both got a hankerin' for Miss Elena, so keep your eyes open.'

The wagon pulled to a halt near the house. The Holders came closer, and Sid started toward Elena, his big black eyes gleaming.

Ben sprang from the wagon and turned to offer his hand up to Elena before Sid could get there. He saw gratitude in her face as she slid her small hand into his.

As she started down, her skirts caught on the seat iron, and she lost her balance. Quickly, Ben reached for her waist, caught her, and lowered her carefully. He liked the feel of her, the gentle weight against his strength. His hands were big at her tiny waist as he set her on the ground. He wanted to hold her a moment, but he saw the sudden stern look on her face. He released her quickly and stepped back. How close he had been. How far away he would forever have to be.

Ben was introduced by his first name, and he was completely ignored. Elena was the main attraction, though she wasn't too happy about it. Gridley's wound was washed and rebandaged.

The Holders insisted on feeding them a hearty supper of beans and bacon. They sat around a hand-hewn table on stools made of tree stumps. Ben savored the bacon.

'They got some hogs in Thunder Valley,' Pa Holder said. 'Them farmers ain't all bad.'

The sons kept fussing around Elena. She seemed uncomfortable but was polite. She had breeding, but it didn't help her with the grubby Holders. There was never a smile on her face, just tolerance.

'We broke them mustangs more'n once,' Sid said. 'They got a lot of fire in 'em. Ole Saul, he ate a lot of dirt.'

'You and me both,' Saul grunted.

Their pa said, 'My boys got guts. They're mighty strong boys too, and handsome under them beards. Why, any lady would be all-fired lucky if they was to come courtin'.'

'Sid even learned to dance,' Saul added.

'If'n we had some music, I'd be mighty pleased to show you, Miss Elena,' Sid remarked, leaning toward her across the table. 'But maybe we don't need no music.'

All the while, Elena sat very erect and proper. She pretended not to hear as she sipped her coffee from the cracked cup.

'Miss Elena can have the bedroom,' Pa Holder said, wiping his mouth with the back of his hand. 'The rest of us can sleep in here, but we gotta take turns on guard. I been seein' smoke in the bluffs.'

'We had a run-in with a bunch,' Gridley said. 'Yavapai, I figure.'

'Don't know about them,' Pa grunted. 'It's Apache we got to watch out for around here. Some Chiricahua broke off from San Carlos and been raidin' south o' here.'

'I can take care o' them Yavapai barehanded,' Saul said, 'but an army ain't enough for one Apache.'

'But don't you worry, Miss Elena,'

Sid said. 'We'll be takin' care o' you.'

Elena forced a small smile and nodded.

Her carpetbag was carried into the back bedroom by Gridley. All three Holders watched with beady eyes. Ben could see the rope bed with its ratty mattress and soiled blankets. There was a very small window on the side wall. It looked protected enough.

Elena bade them good night. Gridley and Ben would take turns sleeping in front of her door. It was going to be a long night.

When Ben had his turn at ranch guard, it was early morning. He moved quietly about the corral area, then returned to the shelter of the front of a shed and settled down in a blanket. The prairie nights were plenty cold. In the distance he heard the call of a lone coyote.

Ben understood that distant cry. All his life he had been hearing it, feeling it, sharing it. He had a mother and brothers he loved, and half brothers

41

and sisters he could love too if they settled down. But he was always lonely, hunting, searching for whatever it was he was missing. Once, he thought he had found it with Caroline.

Just before dawn, Gridley appeared. 'Go on in and get some grub,' he told Ben.

'Don't know what to make of those three fellers.'

'Yes, you do,' Gridley said. 'Watch yourself.'

'You come here often?'

'Whatever else they be, they're plenty good at roundin' up and breakin' them mustangs. We get a lot of our string from 'em. Also, their place makes a good way station when we need to get to the river.'

Ben returned to the adobe house. Inside, Pa Holder was stirring beans in the pan. Oily black coffee was steaming.

Elena appeared from the back room. She looked tired and sleepy, and her hair was tied up in a bun behind her neck. It was as if she were trying to be unattractive.

'Your pa's spread,' Saul said. 'I reckon it keeps growin'.'

'We're surrounded,' she said. 'A few farmers, but mostly small ranchers. And now there's talk of copper in the southern hills.'

'But you keep buyin' more horses,' Sid told her. 'That's got to mean you're hirin' more men.'

'My foreman does the hiring,' she said. 'I'm not involved.'

'You mean ole Gridley?' Saul asked.

'Yes,' she said. 'And he's just hired Ben Darringer.'

She nodded toward Ben, who was drinking his coffee. The Holders paused in their breakfast, gazing at Ben with surprise and suspicion. Saul's eyes narrowed to little dots beneath the lids. Sid wiped his mouth and sneered.

'What for you need a hired gun?' Pa Holder asked. 'You gettin' trouble up there?'

'He don't look so tough,' Sid said,

looking Ben over. 'Them fancy guns don't mean nothin'.'

'That ain't no way to talk to a guest,' his Pa told him. 'Ain't I taught you no manners? You want Miss Elena to think poorly of you?'

Elena folded her napkin. 'I thank you for the use of your wagon,' she said coolly.

As she rose, Ben also stood up. Taking their cue, the Holders stumbled to their feet. Sid's cup spilled over, and coffee ran down the table leg. He clumsily recovered the cup and ignored the spill.

At Elena's request, Ben brought her carpetbag from the bedroom. She turned and walked outside. Ben carried the bag and found it heavy.

Gridley had saddled the horses, and he turned the bay over to Ben. It was a big, tough animal with white streaks on its legs and nose. It snorted and danced as Ben swung astride and took the reins, checking the stirrup length. It was a good fit.

Pausing, he watched Gridley hold the sorrel mare as Elena mounted astride. Only then did Ben notice that her blue skirt was split for riding. It made a lot more sense than a sidesaddle.

'Sure you can handle them mustangs?' Pa Holder asked. 'One of my boys could go along.'

'No, thanks,' Gridley said.

Elena reached into the carpetbag that Gridley held up to her. She drew a small sack and tossed it to Pa Holder, who quickly caught it. He smacked his lips as he drew out one of the gold coins. Then he bit it.

Gridley tied the carpetbag to the rear of her saddle. Then he mounted the sorrel gelding. He and Ben opened the corral gate and brought the mustangs out, circling them as Elena followed. Full of energy, the herd snorted and kicked as they fought to go their own way, but Ben and Gridley managed to get them out of the canyon. Once clear, the travelers breathed more easily.

'I hate going there,' Elena said, not looking back.

Ben rode ahead of the herd, swinging them north. He felt the cool wind in his face. The sun was casting shadows of bluffs on the red earth. The trail to Thunder Valley was shorter now. Farmers, ranchers, Shockley, copper mines. Caroline. There was a lot of trouble awaiting him in Thunder Valley.

46

3

A week had passed since they had left the steamer, and now they were in a pass high in the mountains. Red rocks stood like sentinels on the great walls crested with timber. There was still snow in the shade.

It was their last night on the trail. They huddled close to the fire, the horses roped in against the face of the cliff. The canyon was about forty feet wide here. The walls, rising at least three hundred feet on each side, protected them from the icy wind.

'Feels mighty cold,' Gridley said.

Ben had been glancing at Elena now and then, but she only stared into the flickering flames. She had seemed so delicate around the grizzly Holders. Since then, she had looked as strong and secure as when she had braved Yuma Prison.

'You got kin?' Gridley asked Ben.

'Three brothers, and more family in Texas,' Ben said, wondering why he had answered. But he liked this tough old range rider.

'I got kin back East,' Gridley said. 'They hope they never hear from me, and that's a fact. I'm the bad apple, never accountin' for much.'

'You're holdin' your own.'

'You sure enough studied law?'

Ben nodded. 'With a judge, down in Texas.'

'You figure on goin' back there? You really wanta be a lawyer?'

'Yes.'

'Well, I went to school awhile, till I got run off for fightin'. But I'm beginnin' to think my fightin' days are over. Now I'm just stiff and mean and plumb wore out.'

'I'm a little beat up myself,' Ben said. 'How's your arm?'

'Healin' just fine.'

Ben looked at Elena. She wasn't listening, he was certain. She was staring into the fire as if it were a hearth in a big mansion. He thought of her on the steamer, holding the baby and making it laugh.

He had to remind himself that she held his life in her hands. She could send him back to Yuma with the flick of her little finger. If she didn't get him killed first.

'We'll be comin' to the valley tomorrow afternoon,' Gridley said. 'I'll take the first watch. You'll need your sleep.'

Ben downed his coffee and slipped into his blankets, curling up with his head on his Texas saddle. Weary, he slumbered. He was awakened before dawn. Gridley was muttering.

'I got hair standin' on end,' the old man said. 'Watch yourself.'

Ben took his place at guard. The snorting horses were nervous. Maybe there was a cat up there on the rocks.

He walked over to the ropes keeping in the mustangs. The only sounds he heard were the snorts of the horses and of their hooves digging in the earth. He looked back at the campfire, half hidden in the circle of rocks. It looked peaceful amid the darkness all around.

Time passed. Soon it was nearly dawn. Ben walked about, trying to keep the animals calm. The mustangs were jittery. The cow horses were restless.

The sky was still sprinkled with stars. There was no moon. It was great to be out here, free in the night air. Ben breathed deeply. And then he saw it — the flash of light on the far rock.

Next, the report of a rifle cracked the early morning, and a bullet whistled by his ear. He spun and crashed to the dirt. He crawled on his belly for cover in the rocks near the dancing horses. As another shot rang out, he felt a burn on his left shoulder.

More shots rang out, spitting dirt around the fire. Gridley's bedroll was cut with bullets. Ben wanted to cry out. Elena's bedroll was suddenly riddled too.

50

Ben started to rise up in his fury. Then he saw Gridley crawling on his belly on the other side of the pass. He took a deep breath and kept low. Maybe Elena was safe too.

He lay flat on his middle, trying to get a bead on the flashes of light on the high walls. He raised his Winchester and took a potshot.

A shriek rang out, and a man rose against the pale sky, twisting, staggering, and suddenly falling into space. He crashed against the rocks and smashed like a china doll.

Ben swallowed hard. Bullets hit the dirt around him, and he backed up against the wall and dropped to his knees. That blasted Gridley was using him for bait.

Lying on his back, Ben took aim again, this time at a rock where he was certain that the first shots had come from. He fired at what he thought was a hat.

His shot rang loud in the early light. He fired again when he saw movement.

He heard a yell, then silence.

Gridley was in position across the way. He motioned to Ben to stand up. Drawing a deep breath, Ben sprang to his feet, exposing his whole body to the walls above.

At that moment, two figures rose to get a shot at him from the rim. Before they could fire, Gridley shot one of them. Someone else got the other. Was it Elena?

As the shots echoed in the early light, the horses spun around the rope corral. Ben went over and tried to calm them. There was a long stillness around the travelers. Except for the horses, there was no sound in the pass.

Light began to creep down from the sky.

Now they could see one another and the fallen body more clearly. Ben scanned the ridges above. Either they had them all or some had left.

Gridley moved along the wall, kneeling beside the body. 'You were right, Miss

Elena,' he said. 'It's Jake Miller, one of Walker's men.'

She emerged from the shadows, rifle in hand. Ben felt relief.

Gridley stood up, joined Ben, and helped him calm the horses. He kept his eyes on the cliffs as he spoke.

'I figured somethin' was up. I got Miss Elena up, but made it look like we was still sleepin'.'

'And you used me for bait,' Ben said.

Gridley flashed a crooked smile.

'You've been hurt,' Elena said.

Ben looked down at his blood-streaked shirt. His left shoulder had been hit near the armpit, and now he felt the pain. He walked over to the fire and knelt.

'Bullet just grazed me,' he said.

'We're both lucky, then,' Gridley said.

'Sure ain't no picnic you invited me to,' Ben told him.

Elena picked up a canteen. Then she knelt and ripped Ben's shirt with a small knife. He watched her slim, little fingers as she used a white, lace-trimmed handkerchief to wash away the blood. She rinsed it in water before pressing it to the wound. Her fingers were cold.

She looked up at him. He saw no hostility, but he felt that she didn't see him at all. To her, he was a Colt revolver with a need for a bandage.

Gridley came back and knelt with them as he said, 'Reckon this wasn't such a great place to camp.'

'It has water,' Elena said. 'And a place to hold the mustangs. We always stop here.'

'But I should a listened to the hairs standin' up on the back o' my neck.'

She removed the handkerchief and turned Ben's shoulder toward the light. Her grasp was soft but firm. Again her hand felt cold, without caress. Then she reached into her carpetbag to retrieve a white petticoat. She tore a strip from it.

'Who's Walker?' Ben asked, watching

her bind his shoulder from under the arm.

'Small rancher,' Gridley said. 'One of the troublemakers.'

'You got any law in Thunder Valley?' Ben asked.

'Deputy U.S. marshal comes through about once a year. We got us a small town and a local sheriff, but he don't like mixin' in. Mostly he takes care of the drunks and thieves.'

'If you're looking for help,' Elena said, 'there isn't any.'

He met her gaze, but she looked away quickly.

She sat back several feet away and picked up her coffee cup. Gridley stretched, complaining his body was too beat up for more of this. Yet there was a twinkle in his eye. It was obvious that he liked a good fight.

They buried Walker's man, taking his wallet with his identification. There was ten dollars in it. The wind was still whistling through the canyon. They packed up, saddled, and prepared to leave. They freed the nervous mustangs, allowing them to drink at the nearby creek. Then they headed them out north from the canyon.

Ben liked his bay. It was sure of foot, with powerful muscles that rippled beneath its dark hide. The animal felt good under the saddle. It didn't fight the bit, and it sensed his every command with the reins. Frequently, he reached down to stroke the strong neck.

At noon they were on a high rim of the mountains, riding from the pines and brush into the open. The sky was clear, the wind still cold and insistent. They were approaching Thunder Valley from the south.

On the rim of the mountain, he saw it for the first time. The bottom land was covered with green grass and shrubs and stunted junipers. The earth was red beneath. It was a vast and sprawling valley with rolling hills and a river running east to west. A solid rim of red rock mountain circled the valley, cut only by the river's canyon in the east wall. On top of the rim was a heavy growth of timber. The railroad might build through the canyon.

'That's our valley,' Elena said, leaning on the pommel. 'That's all Barker land on the north side of the Apache River. It's a big river, fed by creeks from all sides.'

'The small ranchers are south of the river,' Gridley added. 'The grass ain't so good there. Off to the east, Shockley's men have moved in right up to the south bank, just darin' us. There's a small fort there, and they figure the soldiers will protect 'em.'

'We don't want to lose any more land,' Elena said. 'The newcomers have backed us up to the river's edge. That's as far as we go.'

They rode down along the rocky trail, keeping the mustangs together as best they could. On the next lower rim, they reined up to view the diggings to their far left.

'Copper,' Elena said. 'They're building a smelter.'

'And there you can see the town,' Gridley said. 'They call it Barkersville.'

Ben pulled down the wide brim of his hat to shade his eyes. He saw the small town along the river in the west, on the south side. There were maybe forty buildings and some shacks.

Gridley said, 'Apache River goes west all the way to the Colorado, but the steamers can't make it up here. They use mules to pull in a keel boat with supplies.'

'Mighty pretty sight,' Ben said.

'We don't fight much over the river,' Gridley said. 'All the herds water there when the creeks are dry. It's the grass we want. We've been reasonable about the south side, which is pretty rocky, but we ain't lettin' 'em cross.'

'Two of our men have been killed,' Elena told Ben. 'Ambushed. Others have been shot at. They want us out or backed right up to the Apache Rim.'

Ben hooked his leg over the pommel

58

and studied the valley, considering all angles. He couldn't see the Barker Ranch, but he figured that they were pretty vulnerable with all that open spread of land.

'We spend more time ridin' the river than herdin' cattle,' Gridley said. 'Come roundup, we'll need eyes in the back of our heads.'

Ben slid his boot back into the stirrup, and they rode along the trail, the mustangs skittish at the narrow edge. The descent took hours, and it was late afternoon when they reached the valley below.

'We ain't stoppin',' Gridley said. 'We'll be fordin' the river in a few hours. Got to get on the other side.'

Ben sensed the tension. Elena was stiff in the saddle, glancing in all directions as they rode. Gridley had his rifle ready at his left leg. Ben drew the Winchester from the scabbard and rested it on the pommel. He was better with his six-guns, but their firing range might not be enough. The land rolled so much that he couldn't see over the next hill.

Gridley picked an unmarked trail. Ben saw no signs of life, no men or cattle, no buildings. Not until they were on a rise looking down on the river. It was twilight. To the far left he could see twinkling lights from the town, maybe ten miles away.

'Only two good places to ford,' Gridley told him. 'Right about here and way down by the fort.'

They crossed the river. Here the clear water was from three to seven feet deep in places. The mustangs took it as if they'd been trained by troopers. The big bay kept abreast of them with ease. Elena's mare had a struggle, but she made it across too. Gridley beat them to the other side.

They were home. Two riders appeared from a grove of shining aspens. They were young cowboys with fresh faces, beardless, bright eyed and grinning, wearing unnecessary chaps for show. They waved them on, and Elena turned in the saddle to look back.

'So young,' she said.

About her own age, Ben thought. But she was right. The boys were too green for a range war. Yet there was a time when he had been just as green and foolhardy.

Darkness was setting in. The rim was black against the pale sky. Night came as they met two other riders. These were aged and crusty, like Gridley. The two men took over the herd.

Soon, they could see the lights of the ranch house. Corrals, sheds, and the bunkhouse were off to the left. It was too dark to make out any other buildings. There were a lot of trees, mostly tall aspen with their shivering leaves. The main two-story house, all timber, was on a knoll that was open to attack. It faced south, toward the river.

The two cowhands took the herd on to the corrals. Ben, Elena, and Gridley reined up at the hitching rail near the porch. It was a grand porch with a fancy railing and a swing. In fact, it was the largest, finest-looking ranch house Ben had seen since leaving Texas. The second floor had its own veranda, and it circled the entire structure.

A great, barren oak stood near the far edge of the veranda. The hill of green grass sloped down in all directions from the home.

'Tomorrow,' Elena said, 'you'll meet my father.'

Gridley swung down to hold her horse as she dismounted. Stiff, she paused to look at them, her eyes glistening in the moonlight. She looked painfully beautiful.

'Thanks, both of you,' she said.

They waited until she was on the porch and into the house. The partially open door revealed a grand parlor with rich maroon furnishings. There was a grand piano in the far corner. Slowly, the door closed on their view of fine living.

Ben sighed at that glimpse of a life he had once sought. As a lawyer, he could have had love, family, some wealth, his own home, children — everything. As a gunfighter, he had only the Colts in his holster and was waiting for the bullet that was faster than his.

'Reckon they have a dozen servants,' Ben said.

'Not likely. Mr. Barker won't eat anything 'less his wife cooks it.'

Ben was surprised, remembering Elena's not helping with the cooking on the trail. Maybe she was particular about whom she served.

'Well, ain't you sleepy?' Gridley asked, back in his saddle.

'Sleepy and plumb sore.'

'Yeah, me too. These old bones ain't much for fightin' anymore. Say, do you play checkers?'

'Reckon so.'

'Tomorrow is Sunday. Maybe we'll have us a game.'

Ben rode with him to the corrals where they unsaddled the horses. The mustangs were in another corral, still not settled down. The night was cold and damp. Ben felt it in his bones. Or was it a premonition of trouble?

As they hung their saddles and bridles on the fence, Gridley told him that they'd make space in the tack room the next day. Both were too weary now for the chore. They had aching wounds that needed healing, and their bodies needed rest.

In the bunkhouse Gridley lit a lamp. The glow through the smoky chimney revealed a typical room lined with bunks and gear. Large enough to be a house, it had a board floor with some cracks. The roof, packed with adobe, had kept it cool. The walls were covered with black, oily paper. A stove was in the corner, barely warm.

The two old cowhands who had brought in the mustangs were already asleep in their long underwear. One of them was snoring away with a slight whistle. The other bunks were empty.

'Some are on watch,' Gridley murmured. 'And some are in town for a Saturday-night hoot.'

He gave Ben a lower bunk on the back wall. Then he pulled off his boots and crawled into the upper bed. Ben started to pull off his boots too, but he hesitated. He was tired, yet restless.

'Stoke the fire,' the older man said.

As quietly as possible, Ben lifted the iron lid, stirred the coals, and shoved in more wood. Then he turned down the lamp. He stood for a moment in the near darkness, savoring the sense of companionship with other men. He had experienced it during the range wars, but he had been the outsider, the hired gun. Watching the men laugh and work together, and then cry and suffer as one, he had envied them.

He would give a lot just now if he could really be one of them. Having a job as a working cowhand meant nothing. He was a fast gun who was supposed to save the store. He would trade his reputation in a minute to be just another weary hand.

He sat on his bunk in the darkness for a long while. Uneasy, unable to settle down, he slipped outside into the moonlight, wearing his old leather jacket. It was cold out, but he wanted to feel the chill. It made him feel alive — and free.

On a far knoll to the south, a night rider was sitting on his horse, outlined by the moon's glow.

Ben walked over to the corral and leaned on the rail as the bay came over to nuzzle him. He stroked the sleek head. The animal pawed the earth.

'Easy, old fella,' Ben said.

As the gelding wandered off, Ben turned to look toward the ranch house. All the lights were out.

Elena was there. She and her family, living well and apart. She had obviously been to finishing school. She spoke well and seemed educated, refined. Like Caroline.

He stiffened abruptly. Smoke. He smelled wood smoke. The slight breeze was blowing to the west, taking the bunkhouse smoke in the other direction, away from him.

It had to be from the ranch chimney, but the house was dark. Maybe they kept a fire in the hearth all night. Maybe not. He hurried around back toward the north side of the house.

From there, he saw the flames racing along the rear wall, for the length of the building.

The house was on fire!

4

With a war whoop, Ben turned and charged like a wild man back to the bunkhouse. He threw open the door and yelled that the house was on fire. Then he raced back across the open ground and up the hill and upon the porch.

He charged the door again and again until the latch broke. Inside, he found the parlor filled with smoke. The fire had broken through the north wall, and he could see the winding stairway with its lush red carpet. It led up to the white-railed veranda where the rooms were.

'Fire!' he shouted.

Flames were furiously eating away the north wall. Velvet curtains were on fire now, and the hungry fire was shooting to the ceiling. He raced to the stairway and ran up three steps at a time, shouting at the top of his lungs.

'Fire! Get out!'

As he reached the landing, he saw an old man coming out of a room with a shotgun. He looked as mean as a grizzly. He was bald and bearded and wore a long nightshirt.

'You're on fire!' Ben called, racing past him to pound on the doors at the north side.

While Ben went in one direction, the man with the shotgun went running in the other. They rattled doorknobs and pounded.

Ben charged a door into a lighted room, and then staggered to a halt as he saw Elena sitting up in a large four-poster bed. She was holding a six-gun in both hands, aimed right at his forehead.

'The house is on fire!' he cried, panting.

Quickly, she sprang out of bed and pulled on a fuzzy blue wrap.

'Let's go,' Ben said.

Shaking her head violently, she rushed to a closet and grabbed an armful of dresses and petticoats. Next she scooped up some shoes and a pair of boots.

Women! he thought, but with appreciation.

She rushed to join him. On the south landing they saw an elderly gray-haired woman in a long white gown coming out of a far room with the old man. She, too, was carrying an armful of clothes. From two other rooms, two men came out hurriedly, pulling on their britches but barefoot. *Tenderfoots*, Ben thought.

Smoke had already filled the parlor, and it rose up and choked them. The northwest end of the upper floor suddenly erupted in flames, blocking a far, windowed door that had to lead to the outside veranda.

'This way,' the old man called.

He led them back through his room. On the way, he grabbed his britches and boots, and then shoved his hat on his head while still carrying the shotgun.

He kicked open a tall, narrow window. With his boot in hand, he knocked the glass clean for them. One by one they climbed out onto the smoky veranda.

The old man helped the women through. The other men followed. The north end of the veranda was in flames. They rushed along the east side toward the front of the house.

The two younger men yelped about splinters on their bare feet. They had slick hair and flat bellies. Their skin was pale, unweathered.

As the group reached the southern front of the house, they could see that the entire west end of the veranda was in flames. The rooms along the south wall were bright with fire. Smoke was pouring up around them.

'Here,' the old man said. 'We'll climb down the tree.'

The tall, lonesome, barren old oak with thick limbs was close to the railing. They lifted the old woman, who was forced to drop her clothes to the ground. She grabbed the limb and worked her way down. It was hard for her, but she didn't hesitate.

Elena, too, had to drop her bundle, shoes, and boots. She leaned way out and grabbed the limb on her own. She nearly lost her grip, but she recovered and started down toward the trunk.

Below, Gridley was waiting to grab the elderly woman and to assist Elena. The two tenderfoots were next, awkwardly swinging into the tree from the rail, one nearly falling. Talking back and forth in Spanish, they were obviously frightened.

Still on the veranda, the old rancher turned to stare at the house. His pain was obvious. He had built this place, furnished it, loved it, and was losing it.

'Go ahead,' the old man grunted, still holding his shotgun.

'You first, Mr. Barker,' Ben said.

'Who are you?'

'Ben Darringer.'

For a long moment, the old man looked Ben over, not missing the twin Colts. He made a face that wasn't complimentary; then he turned and climbed onto the rail and dropped the shotgun to Gridley.

The whole house was in flames now. The veranda was unsteady. Ben heard part of the roof collapse. By now the veranda was shuddering. The old man grabbed for the tree limb just as the flooring gave way.

Ben made a frantic jump, grabbing the same limb as the whole veranda collapsed. Legs swinging back and forth, he hung steady while Barker got his grip and started to slide down the fat, nearly barren limb.

Gridley grabbed the old man and pulled him carefully to the ground. Then he stood back as Ben made his way down and dropped to the earth. The women had already carried their belongings away from the hot, burning house.

They all backed away some forty feet, but they could still feel the heat. The smoke was suffocating.

Everything was going up in flames. One of the cowhands came around the house with a bucket dangling from his hand.

'We tried!' he shouted to Barker over the roar of the fire. 'No sign of the varmints what done it.'

They all backed farther away from the heat, smoke, and ashes. Hot embers floated from the fire, and the men chased and stomped them out.

Moving even farther from the knoll, they stood in the chill of the moonlight and watched the great building collapse little by little, groaning and sighing, often crashing loudly.

Ben glanced at their faces. Barker was grim and mean, his dark eyes gleaming. Mrs. Barker, clutching her silk and velvet gowns, had tears in her pale eyes. Her sweet face was so stricken that Ben wanted to hold her.

Elena stood stiff and erect, tightening

her wrap about her. Her fancy gowns lay at her feet as she watched her home disappear in violent destruction. Her lovely face appeared white, lifeless.

'We'll build it up again,' Gridley said.

'That piano came from St. Louis,' Mrs. Barker said. 'Some of the paintings were priceless.'

'But we're all alive,' Elena said. 'Thanks to Mr. Darringer.'

Mrs. Barker turned, trying hard to smile at Ben. Her husband merely nodded his grudging thanks. Their reaction reminded him that he had killed their only son.

'This is my father and mother,' Elena said to Ben, who tipped his hat to the older woman.

The two dudes hopped about to keep warm in their bare feet. Ben decided that they would be as useful as a pair of goldfish.

Elena said, 'Eduardo Sanchez and his brother Ricardo are visiting us from Mexico.'

Aristocracy, Ben thought. *Breeding. Money. Proper enough to court Elena. But not worth six bits.*

'We'll clear out the bunkhouse,' Gridley said. 'Just give us a few minutes.'

He and the other two hands headed for the out-buildings to make room for the Barkers and their guests. The bunkhouse was the largest structure left.

After a last look at the house, Ben turned to Elena. She was looking directly at him, the fire shining in her dark blue eyes. Her long black hair was lifting slightly in the cold breeze, caressing her shoulders in the blue wrap. A beautiful woman, unreadable, untouchable.

He tipped his hat and followed the other men. Like them, once in the bunkhouse, he made up his bedroll. They would have to crowd in the tack room and sheds tonight. It would be hard to find spare boots for the dudes.

Coming back out of the bunkhouse, he looked at the fiery remains of the great home on the knoll. He hated to see it die before his eyes.

The women were first in the bunkhouse. Barker paused at the doorway and said to Ben, 'I sure hope you're as fast as they say you are.'

'Mr. Barker,' Gridley said, 'I saw Ben runnin' and fightin' and never missing a shot.'

'So my daughter said,' the rancher grunted. 'Seems like you saved her from them Injuns. And now I guess you sure enough saved us from being burned up. I gotta thank you.'

Ben nodded but didn't answer. Without offering his hand, Barker turned away. The two dudes were carefully walking up to the building.

'You'll bed down in the tack room,' Barker told them. 'My womenfolk are in here.'

Ben was kind of pleased as the barefoot men hopped and skipped all the way to the distant building by the corral. Two cowhands headed for the trees to stand guard.

Gridley looked from the bunkhouse to the dudes on their way to the tack room. He shook his head.

'Got to be some place better.'

'What's that other shack?' Ben asked.

'Smithy. It's got only three walls but a good roof. And a fire pit.'

After a meal over an open fire, served by an old cowhand, they turned toward the smithy. They paused to take another look at the shuddering remains of the great house. Silently, they walked on to the distant shed near the far corrals.

When they arrived there and had spread out their bedrolls inside the three walls, Ben sat down and said to Gridley, 'There are other gunfighters from Texas to the Dakotas. How is it they set so much store on my reputation?'

'There were a lot of tall tales from Texas at your trial. A few of them were brought in by some new hands.

And some feller in Barkersville said as how you're the only one can take Zevala.'

Ben turned cold, right to his gut. 'Zevala?'

'He's comin', I hear. Shockley's bringin' him in.'

'Well, just for your hearin', I'm not sure I could take Zevala.'

'This feller in Barkersville said — '

'What feller?' Ben asked.

'Big, slick feller. Name's Clay Smith, he says. Gambler, I think. Wears a beard and has a white scar on his left cheek. Says he got it from an Apache down near the Mexican border. He's got a lot of stories, some a little farfetched. Tall talker, that one.'

It must be his brother Clay. Clay was here, just a few miles away. His brother had been bragging that Ben could take Zevala. Well, it sure worked. The Barkers were so afraid of the Texas killer that they were taking a chance on getting him out of jail, all the while hating him for killing one of their own. Now it made sense why they wanted him.

'Yeah, you'll like Smith,' Gridley said, stoking the fire in the iron pit. 'You don't know him?'

'Not likely.'

'He claims he saw you in gunfights down in Texas. Swears you're the only one could take Zevala.'

'Sure hope he's right.'

But Ben was excited. He hadn't seen Clay since he'd helped him and Hank escape so long ago. He sure wanted to see him again.

'I posted a guard,' Gridley said. 'You won't have any trouble with the men. Every one of 'em hates Walker and they'd all die for old man Barker.'

'Are they gun hands?' Ben asked.

'Only two gun hands on this here ranch — you and Mr. Barker. He used to be plenty fast.'

'What about the dudes?' Ben asked.

'Mrs. Barker is bound and determined that Elena should marry well. Reckon the Sanchez brothers are highfalutin

80

folks down in Mexico, but they ain't good for much. They ride like they was sittin' on a fence.'

'You reckon Elena will do what she's told?'

'It's bred in her, son. But like I say, she ain't for the likes of you, though I'm beginnin' to think she couldn't do much better.'

Lying in a dark corner of the smithy, Ben chewed the man's words. It was a compliment, all right, but it was just talk. He had killed her brother, and her family would certainly feel that she was too good for a gunfighter. But he was through with women, so it didn't really matter.

Curling up in his blankets, Gridley was soon asleep and breathing heavily. Ben was restless, and he sat up to stare toward the embers of the great house. The Barkers had lost a great deal.

Ben had come here only to be free, to earn the pardon. But he was beginning to side with the Barkers. An enemy that would burn a man's home with his women in it was Ben's enemy as well. He thought of Jess's words: 'The Darringers always have to get in the middle of things. We can't never be neutral.' Jess was right. He didn't feel one bit neutral about the fire or the arsonists.

He turned and looked at the bunkhouse. There was a soft glow at the window. The women were probably afraid to sleep. But at least they had their clothes. The thought made him grin a little. He was glad that women were different.

Finally he turned in, weary from the two fights on the trail and the frantic rush through the burning house. He felt drained. He smiled as he drew up his blankets. Soon he would see Clay. And Jess would be coming with the Shockley herd, right along with Zevala. His smile faded as he thought of Caroline, who would probably be riding with them.

'I'll always love you,' she had whispered one evening on her porch swing. 'There'll never be anyone else.'

Bitterness returned, and he fell asleep.

And while he slept, the Barkers were trying to make themselves comfortable in the bunkhouse. Isabella Barker, her aged body just as creaky as the bunks, was having difficulty, but she was determined to make the best of it. There would be no protection from her husband's terrible snoring, but she wanted to be close to him tonight.

Jack Barker, mumbling to himself about their enemies, was checking the shotgun. Fury was still written in red all over his face. He was never too old to hate.

'It's all right, Jack,' his wife said. 'We'll build a new house. It'll be just as beautiful.'

'But it ain't right,' he growled, setting his shotgun aside and checking his scratched arms.

Elena came to kneel by her mother and cover her more closely with the heavy blankets.

'I feel something crawling on me,' the old woman said.

'Try to sleep,' Elena said. 'At least we're alive.'

'Yes,' her mother said. 'Thanks to Ben Darringer.'

'Don't you be gettin' soft,' Barker said. 'We can't never forget he shot our boy. He's nothin' but a killer.'

'I'm not so sure,' Elena said.

'Now don't you start,' Barker grunted.

'He could have let us die in the fire,' Elena argued.

'Sure, and never get you to sign for his pardon,' her father reminded her. 'He needs us just like we need him. But when this is over, I got a spot all picked out for him on boot hill.'

'And how will you do it?' his wife asked. 'Shoot him in the back? An ambush? You know you can't do that. I don't want to lose you the way we lost our son. It's too dangerous, Jack.'

'Maybe we won't be worryin' about

it,' Barker said. 'It could be that Zevala takes him.'

'I pray not,' his wife said. 'Ben Darringer is all that stands between us and the rest of the valley.'

Elena lay back on a bunk as her father turned down the lamp. Wood crackled in the stove. She was still cold, and she was tired and sad about the loss of their home. Her father could replace things with money, but something peaceful and grand had died in that fire.

Her mother said in the semidarkness, 'Don't you think that Eduardo and Ricardo were terribly brave?'

'Yes, mother,' Elena said softly.

But she wasn't thinking of the two visitors. She was remembering how Ben had come charging into her room. Even at the sight of her six-gun trained on him, he had not hesitated. Uneasily, she thought of the Yavapai fighting to carry her away. Ben had come charging across the open space like a wild man, firing on the run. She had never seen anything like it. She could still feel his arms as he lifted and carried her to the campfire.

Binding his wound after the attack in the canyon, she had sensed his steady gaze on her face as she tied the bandages. He had been a man then, not a hired gun, and not the man who had killed her only brother.

When she went to sleep, she saw Ben's face, his gray eyes and his big, strong hands. She was beginning to wish she had never met him.

While Elena tossed and turned, Ben was dreaming of his brothers and of Caroline. Only briefly did he see Elena, sitting up in her bed with her six-gun aimed at him. She had looked beautiful. He mumbled in his sleep, waking himself up.

It was first light. He sat up, realizing he had not been asked to take a turn at guard. The ranch hands had likely allowed both him and Gridley to rest up. Ben didn't mind. He was still stiff and weary.

Gridley snored suddenly. The sound startled the old man, and he grunted himself awake. Sitting up clumsily, he looked around.

'What the devil was that?'

'Just you,' Ben said, grinning. 'You snore like a brayin' donkey.'

'Ain't true,' the foreman grunted.

They watched the dudes walking toward the remains of the house. They wore borrowed boots and shirts over their tight britches. Barker was already at the ruins, kicking at the ashes. It was a sad sight.

Then Mrs. Barker came from the bunkhouse, wearing one of her fine silk dresses, blue, with lace at the collar. She was having trouble walking. Probably she was stiff and sore from the climb down the tree. She joined her husband and took his arm as he moved back from the ruins.

Ben looked back at the bunkhouse, waiting for Elena to appear. She didn't.

'Let's get movin',' Gridley said. 'I don't figure them mustangs are all that broke. Can you sit a bronc?'

Ben nodded, then rose to his feet.

The two cowhands who had shared the tack room with the dudes were staggering out just as several riders appeared on a southern rise.

'That be the boys comin' back from town,' Gridley said.

There were six of them, heavy in the saddle, drooping.

'Are ten riders all we got?' Ben asked. 'These two, the six ridin' in, and the two youngsters down by the river?'

'Two more outriders make twelve. Two others got killed. But don't you worry none. We got a dozen more comin' for roundup. And now that we got Ben Darringer, it'll be easier to hire some more.'

As the six fumbled off their horses, Ben looked them over. Two were young, four were oldtimers, and all were in bad shape. But they looked like good men.

When Gridley introduced them to

Ben, they seemed impressed.

Then Gridley told them about the fire and how no one was hurt. The men were sad and furious about the cowardly attack on the family. It was obvious that they had admired the grand house and were loyal to the Barkers.

Ben and Gridley stood by as the cowhands unsaddled, corraled their horses, and fed them some oats. These men were in terrible condition, some barely able to stand.

One of the young men wiped his boyish face. 'We sure had a hoot down in Barkersville,' he said. 'They got a new saloon girl. Real pretty, and friendly too.'

'She ain't as pretty as that lady we saw,' the other youth said. 'You know, the one in the carriage.'

'Yeah, you mean the one who's gonna marry a Shockley.'

Ben's mouth was dry as he heard the words. They had to be talking about Caroline. She was here, ahead of the herd, waiting for Shockley. Once, she had been waiting for him, her promise soft on her lips.

She didn't know his brother Clay, so she couldn't give him away. But she was here, less than twenty miles away. He wasn't ready for her or Zevala.

5

It was Sunday morning. The sky was clear, the air set with chill. Ben shaved and washed at the trough, using the hand pump that drew water from the nearby well. He stretched and gazed around the ranch.

Some of the men were in the corral with the mustangs, looking them over, preparing to ride some of them to see if they were still green. A few animals were running around as if they'd never felt a rope.

In one of the distant sheds and corral, there was a short, fat, white-faced bull. Ben walked over to lean on the fence and study the plump rascal. He agreed with Gridley. The bull would have one heck of a time with the tall, rank longhorns.

But times were changing. The West was getting civilized, like Jess had said.

There would soon be no room for a lone rider.

He turned around and walked back to the tack room, where Gridley was soaping his saddle in the shade of the building.

On the knoll, the black ruins lay grim in the sunlight. The big, barren tree had been charred, but its limbs still hovered above the ground. The aspens circling the house had barely been singed.

He looked around the valley. Apache Rim circled it as far as he could see, a great sandstone and rock formation of white and crimson, topped with pine forests. It rose hundreds of feet from the valley floor.

To the south, he could see the shimmering aspens that lined part of the river, but he couldn't see the water. The grass was mostly green, sometimes poking up through red earth with great effort, and in other places spread in great, wondrous sweeps.

He stood near Gridley and leaned

on the corral as he talked to the old cowhand.

'One thing struck me funny. When a ranch gets on fire, the neighbors will usually come riding to help fight it. And they'd be by the next day with food and clothing.'

'Well, this has got to tell you how well the Barkers are liked around here, seein' as how we got all the good grass and money enough to buy anything we need.'

They watched as a buckboard came around the bunkhouse. It was driven by one of the young cowboys and pulled by a team of blacks. Barker came out in borrowed clothes. The two women followed him, dressed in their finery.

'Church,' Gridley said.

Ben had to get to town to see Clay. He fought the urge to invite himself to church. Resting his hands on his six-guns, he watched as the buckboard was loaded and came their way.

Barker was driving, a rifle resting against his knee. His wife sat next to

93

him, and Elena was on the edge of the creaking wagon seat.

Barker stopped near Ben and Gridley and glared down at them. He looked as mean as sin as he growled, 'Don't suppose either o' you wants to join us for church.'

'Ben oughta go,' Gridley said. 'Just in case Shockley's sent some men there. I hear a fiancée of one of his sons just arrived in town. And I'll send young Jenson along.'

Elena avoided Ben's gaze as he agreed to go. They started on ahead with the wagon while he went to saddle his bay. As he mounted, the big animal danced, full of demon energy.

Jenson, one of the fresh young men, wore a tied-down six-gun, and he looked as if he could handle himself rather well. He brought out his sorrel, already saddled, and swung astride.

'Watch yourselves,' Gridley said.

Ben set his mount to a lope, Jenson following suit. Soon they were riding at a walk behind the wagon as the

Barkers headed south to the river. It was a clear, crisp day. After a while, Jenson rode on ahead to scout the river area. Ben stayed to the rear, keeping his eyes open. The rolling country had only scattered groves of aspen and juniper, but each knoll hid the next hollow from view. Overhead, two black buzzards floated on the wind.

At Apache River Jenson crossed first, and then Barker half drove, half floated the wagon across. Ben swam his bay over to join them. He kept to the rear, letting Jenson ride point.

Elena was sitting very erect. Her long black hair, swept into rolls, was bound by a blue ribbon that matched her velvet jacket and dress. Her mother wore a green silk dress. Ben had to admire them. They had lost their home to a deliberately set fire. Yet they were determined to show the whole town that they were not afraid.

Moving along the shallow river, Ben estimated that it was mostly sixty feet across. In places, the red bottom-earth colored the cold, fast-moving water. Snow had to be melting in the mountains, somewhere beyond the rim.

He could see the town ahead now, rambling buildings and corrals spread on a hill alongside the river. There was a boat dock at the foot of a long ramp. There could have been a ferry crossing here, but the Barkers were probably refusing access to their side of the river.

The large, two-story building had to be the local hotel. As they entered the town, he saw the livery to the left. It was a big barn with a few horses and mules in a back corral. The ground in the main street was uneven, with some mud holes full of water.

The big hotel on the left, past the barber shop, was in need of paint after a hard winter. It had a big glass window and a covered porch, giving guests a view of the river. Past it were the general store, a barber shop, and other establishments.

On the north side of the street,

near the ramp to the dock, was a saloon. Laughter was coming from inside. Maybe Clay was in there.

As people came out of stores and the hotel, they watched the Barkers drive on through. The Barkers looked straight ahead. A hastily constructed jail looked empty on the right. Next to it, a stone building had a sign saying Barkersville Bank.

On another hill, to the left and just beyond the edge of town, there was a wooden structure with a cross on the roof. Several wagons and many horses were outside. Ben could hear organ music and singing drifting out of the building.

Jenson reined back to ride next to Ben.

'Mr. Barker paid for that there church,' the youth said. 'He even brought in the organ, all the way from St. Louis.'

They reined up, and Ben watched as Barker slid down to help his womenfolk dismount over the big front wheel.

Barker and his wife didn't look back as they walked toward the entrance, but Elena paused and looked up at Ben.

'Please come in,' she said.

She was serious, her blue eyes dark. For some reason, she was worried, even about church. She turned and followed her parents.

Ben was confused by this woman. Caroline had always been soft, feminine, and helpless. Elena could use a rifle like a man, had had no tears when she shot one of Walker's men, and could swallow her fear in battle. Yet he had seen a softness in her when she wasn't aware of his scrutiny.

'I'll keep an eye on the horses,' Jenson said. 'I can't sing nohow.'

Ben swung down, conscious of his six-guns even though Barker had carried his rifle inside. He followed the family, but he was getting nervous. Not about their enemies. He could face men with guns. But Caroline could be in there.

He stepped inside and remained near

the door. The Barkers had moved into the empty rear pew on the right.

There were at least fifty people in the church. Most of the men were wearing sidearms. The women wore everything from sunbonnets to ribbons in their hair. Their dresses ranged from homespun to store-bought. No one was dressed as elegantly as the Barker women.

The congregation was singing 'Rock of Ages.' Ben joined in while he looked for Caroline. She and her family never missed a service. She had to be here.

The music ended and everyone else was sitting down. Ben lowered himself upon a chair near the door. The timber frame of the church was sealed with clay. The altar was a simple table before a wooden cross on the wall. However, the pastor was wearing a full black robe with a huge golden cross on a chain. He was a little man with sharp eyes.

The service was familiar to Ben. It was like being home in Texas, his mother fussing because her boys were too restless.

He couldn't help looking for Caroline. He spotted a woman in the front row with yellow hair done up in fancy curls. Maybe it was she.

The pastor was into his sermon, and his voice rose:

'There's a great sin in this valley. It's the sin of greed, greed for cattle, water, and grass. Greed for wealth. All of you are guilty of this sin. You all want something more than you've earned.'

When the pastor paused, the room was so silent that Ben could hear his own breathing. Glaring at his congregation, the pastor held up the Bible, trying to lead them back to the straight-and-narrow path.

When the service was finally over, everyone rose for the final hymn. Afterward, the pastor strode forward to be at the door to greet them as they filed out. He cast a surly glance at Ben's twin Colts.

Feeling sweat on his face, Ben

watched the people in the front rows exiting first. Several couples and children passed by, all staring at him.

And there she was — Caroline! She was accompanied by an old woman in gray. But Caroline was pink faced and pretty in a lace-trimmed gown that matched her golden hair. Her light blue eyes were glistening until she saw Ben.

'Oh,' she gasped.

Pausing, she stared at him in dismay. The old woman, sharp eyes gleaming, hurried her past him, but Caroline looked over her shoulder, still aghast. And why not? She thought he was in prison for life. Maybe she would remember how she had deserted him the moment he was arrested.

Ben lost sight of her as others filed past. He didn't know what he felt. Shaken, he didn't know if it was love or regret.

The Barkers were the last to leave. Mrs. Barker looked proud and stubborn. Her husband just looked mean. Despite her stern composure, Elena seemed tired. The bunks couldn't have been as comfortable as her feather bed.

He followed them outside. People were standing around and chatting. No one came to tell the Barkers they were sorry about their ranch house. Even the pastor merely shook their hands. He apparently saw them as the cause of all the evil.

Turning to Ben, the pastor looked up at him grimly.

'And you are?'

'Ben Darringer.'

'And why are you here?'

Elena turned around. 'He's our new hand.'

'A new hand?' a big woman spouted, glaring at them. 'He's a gunfighter. He's here because Zevala is coming. There's going to be a bloody war, and we merchants are going to be caught right in the middle.'

Standing taller and more proud, Elena spoke clearly:

'You merchants are here because my

father made room for you in this valley. He's lent money to you. Some has never been repaid. He's always been there to help. Now that he's in trouble, you can only think of yourselves.'

'Now listen, Miss Barker,' said a small man with cropped hair. 'We know what we owe your pa, but he's too blamed stubborn. Why does he need all the grass in the valley? The small ranchers like Walker have also got a right to be here.'

'No one has a right to be here,' Elena said, 'but my family. You know very well that they have a land grant.'

'Well, you ain't heard nothin' from Washington on that,' the big woman said, her red face wrinkling. 'Meanwhile, you're building up a range war.'

'We're standing fast,' Elena said. 'It's the others who are crowding us. On the trail back from Yuma, they tried to shoot me and two of our men. Last night they burned down our home. We almost died in the fire. Who has a right to do that?'

It was then that she saw the sheriff standing there. He was a paunchy, round-faced, lazy-mannered man with a star on his tan vest. He tipped his hat to her and started to walk away.

'Just a minute, Sheriff,' Elena said. 'Aren't you going to do something about it?'

'Out of my jurisdiction,' he said coldly. 'Mine ends right down there, other side of the livery.'

'Well, at least,' Barker said, 'you can return this wallet to Walker. One of his men ambushed my daughter.'

The sheriff looked confused, but he took the leather wallet and shoved it into his inside pocket.

Elena was fuming. Her mother took her arm, trying to calm her, silently reminding her that she was a lady. Her father, however, looked mighty proud of her.

The sheriff turned and hurried away. The big woman sniffed and spun about while a small man took her arm. The others stared and backed away. Elena turned to the pastor.

'Don't *you* have anything to say?'

'I'm sorry about your home,' the little man said. 'All I want is to avoid any more killing. As long as the Barkers hold all the good land north of the river, there's going to be trouble.'

'We're holding that land,' Barker said.

As people walked or drove away, Ben looked for Caroline. There was no sign of her. He felt as if he had hot chili in his belly. She had brought all the hurt back to life.

The pastor went inside the church.

'I see that Walker ain't showed his face,' Barker said.

'Jack,' his wife said, 'we have to get to the store. We need almost everything.'

As the Barkers climbed onto the buckboard, Mr. Barker told Ben that they would be in town a few hours. Looking forward to a reunion with Clay, Ben watched the family wagon roll down the hill toward the center of town.

He and Jenson mounted and rode on down to the main street, where they reined up in front of the saloon. The Barkers had stopped at the hotel, which was next to the general store. Leaving their horses tied at the railing, Ben and the young cowhand went into the saloon.

There were a dozen men lounging about, some playing poker, others at the bar. A bald little man was plunking out 'Red River Valley' on a piano. Some of the men looked curiously at Ben.

There was one woman, blond, frail but comely, painted and tired looking. She wore an ankle-length red dress, her shoulders bared. Next to her, with his back to Ben and Jenson, was a big man with broad shoulders, wearing a leather jacket. His dark brown hair was cropped at the collar, and his hat was brown and weathered. His rifle rested on the walnut bar.

Ben tightened inside. He was glad when Jenson saw a friend and headed over to a far table. Walking to the bar, Ben stopped on the other side of the woman.

As he ordered some of the apple cider from the big jug, he turned and his gaze met Clay's. They looked at each other a long, fond moment. It had been over a year since their previous meeting, and Ben wanted to hurry over and hug his brother.

The girl was talking to Clay, her back to Ben.

'My, you really are a tall one. Can you dance?'

'Not on Sunday,' Clay said, his mustache twitching.

'Over there,' Ben said, nodding toward Jenson. 'That young feller can dance up a storm.'

She turned and smiled up at Ben. 'Hi, stranger.'

'You're plenty fickle,' Clay observed.

'I'm the only woman here,' she said. 'Why not?'

They watched her sway across the room and plunk down on the knee of a startled Jenson. Ben moved a few steps closer to Clay as he sipped the cider. Clay was having some of the same. No one had dared comment.

'You one of the ranchers here?' Ben asked.

'No, I'm just passin' through. Cards are my trade. Care to take a hand?'

'Sure. There's an empty table in the back corner there.'

They took up their glasses and walked casually to the table, where they sat down with their backs to the wall. Clay took out a beaten deck of cards and shuffled it.

'That deck marked?' Ben asked.

'No need,' Clay said. As he grinned, the white scar twisted on his left cheek. His big hands were adept as he dealt five-card stud.

'It's sure good to see you,' Ben said, his voice low.

'Clay Smith, that's my name. So the Barkers went ahead and busted you out. I painted you up pretty well. I told 'em you were the only one who could take Zevala. They hate your guts, but they need you.'

'I stick a year before I can get a pardon.'

'Don't trust 'em, Ben.'

'You ever seen this Zevala?'

'Yeah, I have. He'd as soon gut you as look at you. I figure he's got to be half Mexican or Comanche and half Irish. But he's too confident.'

Ben leaned back in his chair. It was good to see his brother. He thought back to the days when the four of them were riding free.

'You seen Hank?' Ben asked.

'Not since you busted us out. We both split in opposite directions, me to Mexico and him up to the Dakotas.'

'When this is over, we could look for him.'

'I'd like that. One tale I heard, he was wearin' a different name and a badge.' Clay added, 'What about Jess?'

'Gabby as ever. He came to see me in prison. He's comin' here with Shockley's herd.'

'One of Shockley's women is here,' Clay said.

'I know. Caroline Frost. Promised to Rich Shockley, I hear.'

'So you know her?'

'She's the only woman I ever wanted to marry. As soon as I was arrested, she turned her back on me.'

Ben downed his drink and leaned back in his chair, trying to appear nonchalant.

'I heard the Barkers' house was burned down last night,' Clay said with a frown.

'Mighty fine house too,' Ben said. 'I figure the shootin' will start when Shockley moves in with his herd. South of the river, the grass is pretty thin. He'll be tryin' to cross over.'

'Watch yourself. Zevala works alone, Ben, but he likes to put on a show. I figure that's his weakness.'

Ben was tired of talking about his

own troubles. He folded his arms and smiled at his brother. 'What about you, Clay? I haven't seen you in quite a spell.'

'Well, I went first to Mexico. Met a girl and got married. She and our baby died in childbirth. I sorta drifted after that. Did some trackin' for the Army. California for a while. Then I heard you were in Yuma Prison. I came to Arizona to find out why.'

The blond woman was laughing, trying to drag Jenson to his feet as the piano played a lively 'Turkey in the Straw.'

'They were playin' that song down in Texas, remember?' Clay said. 'Right across the street from the jail, same night you busted us out.'

'If I get this pardon, I'm going back to Texas. I'm going to try to clear your names.'

'I reckon that our trouble is what got you where you are. Right sorry about that, Ben.'

'You'd have done the same for me.'

'But you gave up law.'

'And you gave up medicine,' Ben reminded him.

Barker appeared in the doorway and looked around. Jenson saw him and freed himself from his admirer. Ben stood up slowly, tossing down his hand of cards.

'Well, mister,' he said, 'I reckon you won that one.'

'I'll back your play,' Clay murmured. 'Any time.'

Ben walked over to Barker and Jenson, and they moved out into the sunlight. It was warm and windless. Barker led the way across the street to the buckboard outside the hotel. The bed was loaded with goods.

'I tried to get the women to stay in town a few days,' Barker said to Ben, 'but they're too stubborn. Tell 'em we're ready, will you? They're in the hotel.'

Barker climbed onto the wagon seat and took up the reins. While Jenson went for the horses, Ben went reluctantly into the hotel. He was afraid he would see Caroline.

The lobby was pleasantly decorated with blue and white furniture. The desk was ornate, with a bent old man behind it. Two women were seated on a couch near the far wall. They had their noses in the air.

Mrs. Barker was coming from a back room. She never smiled, Ben thought. She was too aristocratic, attempting to carry on tradition, determined to win. Elena was behind her.

'Mr. Barker's waiting,' Ben told them.

'Elena, I forgot my shawl,' the old woman said, and she continued past Ben as if he weren't there.

As Elena went back into the other room, Ben followed her. They were alone. She turned, startled to see him.

'Your father is right,' he said. 'It would be safer for you and your mother to stay here.'

She picked up the heavy shawl, gazing at him oddly. 'My mother

113

would never do that.'

'What about you?'

'I'm not afraid, now that you're here.'

She said it matter-of-factly, but her eyes were more friendly than usual. Ben stood aside as she started past.

'I'm only one man, Miss Elena.'

'It takes only one to get Zevala. That would break them down, destroy their confidence, and make Shockley stop and think.'

He walked behind her, gritting his teeth. In the lobby, something made him pause. He saw Elena walking across to the entrance, but he couldn't move. Slowly, he turned and gazed up the winding staircase.

On the landing, away from view of anyone but him, Caroline was standing. She was signaling to him, asking him to come up the stairs.

Ben's heart fell to his feet. He couldn't move.

6

At the doorway, Elena had paused and was waiting for Ben. He drew a deep breath, turned, walked toward her, and followed her outside. He didn't look back, but his heart was heavy.

The midafternoon sun was bright and warm, and the street was busy now, full of wagons and riders, and dogs and children. As Ben met Jenson with the horses behind the wagon, he paused to watch Barker helping his women aboard. The wagon was pointed east, toward home.

At that moment, a buckboard came rattling up the street toward them, headed west, but it pulled to a halt alongside the Barkers. Its occupants were the dirty, bearded, black-eyed Holders. Pa Holder was grinning through his whiskers.

'Hello there, Mr. Barker. And Mrs.

Barker,' he said. 'We'll be in town a spell. And my boys, they're comin' courtin'.'

Ben couldn't see Barker's face, but he saw his body stiffen. Elena and her mother were looking straight ahead.

Pa Holder wasn't discouraged. ''Course, they'll be cleanin' up a bit,' he said. 'Maybe even get a few new duds.'

'Don't worry about our ranch none,' Saul said. 'We done cleared out till the Apache scare is over.'

'About thirty of 'em prowlin' the area,' Sid told them.

'We wasn't scared much,' Pa Holder said, 'but it was time we had us a little fun.'

The Holders looked at Ben as he mounted. Sid and Saul leaned forward on the wagon seat. They grinned.

'Well, if it ain't the fast gun,' Sid remarked.

Stiff as a board, Barker turned slowly to glare at the men. His voice was gritty as he spoke: 'Holder, you and your sons are welcome in town, but they ain't comin' courtin'.'

'Well,' Pa Holder said, undaunted, 'you'll change your mind as soon as my boys are all cleaned up. They'll be mighty handsome. And I learned 'em some manners too.'

'Keep 'em off my land,' Barker growled. He slapped the reins on the horses, grunted something, and headed the wagon up the street. The Holders said a cheerful good-bye and continued in the other direction, not one bit discouraged.

Ben and Jenson followed the Barkers toward the edge of town. As he passed the saloon, Ben was glad that he had seen Clay and that Caroline had never met his brother. Only Ben knew who the big man in the saloon was.

He turned in the saddle and looked back to the hotel. The old hurt was still there. And maybe the old love was there too. At one point, as he rode alongside the wagon, he looked up at Elena. She was on the end of the seat, sitting very proper and erect. She glanced at him, her eyes neither friendly nor hostile. What had Clay said? 'They hate your guts.'

Ben had killed the Barkers' only son. Clay was right. Jess was right. That pardon was an illusion. Once he had done his job, they would either have him shot or send him back to Yuma. But he was determined, one way or another, to survive.

The wagon and escort followed the river to the crossing. Arriving in late afternoon, they floated and swam across to the north side. Two riders came to greet them.

'No trouble all day,' one said.

The party continued to the ranch, where everything was unloaded at the bunkhouse.

'I don't want them Holders on this place!' Barker roared.

'They can't be serious about my little girl,' his wife said.

'They're very serious,' Elena said. 'They frighten me.'

'Don't you worry none,' her father told her. 'I'll blast 'em right out of the saddle if they ever come foolin' around here.'

Ben carried the last of the clothing bundles into the bunkhouse. He wanted to tell Barker that he'd be right there beside him. Ben was not about to let those grubby men anywhere near Elena.

Some of the food sacks were carried off to the tack room for the men. It was twilight, peaceful.

Then Gridley came over, looking grim. His handlebar mustache twitched as he faced Barker. The old rancher paused, knowing that his foreman had something serious to say. Even the women paused near the open door of the bunkhouse.

'Mr. Barker,' the cowhand said, 'I got some bad news. When we went to feed the new bull this afternoon — well, I got to tell you, it's dead. Someone got in there and cut its throat.'

Barker was stunned, and his face became red with anger. The women looked equally upset, but were silent.

'Dirty buzzards!' Barker snarled. 'Good thing I didn't see Walker in town.'

'Another thing,' Gridley said. 'I got word that the Shockley herd is just a few days out of the valley. They'll be getting to the Shockley spread right soon.'

Shockley . . . Jess . . . Zevala. Ben could hardly wait to tell Jess that their brother Clay was in town. He was in no hurry for the rest, especially Zevala.

'Been a long day,' Barker said to his women. 'Why don't you go on inside? I got some planning to do.'

Elena and her mother hesitated, then went into the bunkhouse. Barker gathered his men over by the tack room. The two dudes stood back and listened.

'Now, you fellas all know that Darringer here is pretty fast with a gun,' Barker said. 'I guess you know, too, that we're in for a fight. There are twelve of you, plus Gridley and Darringer, and we got about twelve more hired for the roundup. They'll be here in a week or so. With twenty thousand head of cattle, we're gonna have our hands full.'

'You think the Shockleys will try to cross the river?' one man asked.

'I figure the fire was done by Walker, because it's the coward's way,' Barker said. 'But I don't reckon Shockley to be one bit shy. He's gonna hit us hard, probably in broad daylight.'

'What have *you* got to say, Darringer?' a man asked.

'I heard about Shockley in Texas,' Ben said. 'He's not bashful, but I figure he'll take his time till he's got the upper hand. He'll get the lay of the land first.'

'Another thing,' Barker said. 'I want every one of you to be on the lookout for them mustangers, the Holders. I don't want them around here.'

When the talk was over, Barker

returned to the bunkhouse. The men had their grub over an open fire and then bedded down for the night. The Sanchez brothers were still crowding everyone in the tack room. Gridley and Ben retreated to the smithy by themselves.

'You find that Smith feller?' Gridley asked.

'Yes, but he isn't anyone I know.'

'How was it, goin' to church?'

'Crowded,' Ben said. 'You should have heard Miss Elena tell the folks off, including the sheriff.'

'Right proud of that lady,' Gridley said. 'If I was a few years younger, I'd be sittin' on her porch.'

'Are they going to rebuild the house?'

'Sure enough, when the roundup is over. After we get them new calves and mavericks branded, we'll be drivin' 'em for sale to the Army. And in a few months we'll be cuttin' timber.'

'Meanwhile, the Barkers stay in the bunkhouse?'

'They're mighty proud folks, Ben.

You'll learn that soon enough.'

Ben had already seen their pride in Elena's flashing eyes and the tongue-lashing she gave the church crowd and the sheriff.

He helped Gridley build up a fire in the pit, and then they spread out their blankets. The sky was full of stars. It was cold, but Ben was content. Anything was better than Yuma.

Gridley was sound asleep when a young cowhand came up quietly and shook Ben, who was still awake.

'Got a letter for you,' he said. 'From a fine lady in town. She said I wasn't to give it to anyone but you.'

Ben sat up, staring at the envelope in the dim firelight. His name was written in a soft, delicate hand — Caroline's.

He waited until the cowhand was gone. Then he walked over to the fire. His bitterness made him hesitate to open the letter. He had an urge to toss it into the flames.

The year he spent in that wretched cell had included many hours berating her. And yet, the envelope was as soft as her hand.

Taking a deep breath, he broke the seal and drew out the piece of pink paper. He felt cold fingers gripping his middle as he read the words.

Dear Ben,

If you only knew how heartbroken I was when my parents rushed me out of Tucson. My uncle was with me. I couldn't even write to you. Then I heard you were convicted and going to prison. I knew I would never see you again. When my parents matched me with Richard Shockley, I didn't even care. But now that you're free, I feel that I'm alive again. I must see you. Please come to town or send word how to meet you.

All my love,
Caroline

Staring at the words, Ben wasn't sure what to believe. She was almost twenty, not a helpless child. He told himself that if she had really wanted to get word to him, she could have.

He thought of Elena, who seemed afraid of no one. But, then, Caroline had led a sheltered life and needed a man's guidance and protection. He was torn in his thoughts.

He folded the letter and placed it in his pocket. It weighed heavily. He lay back in his blankets and stared at the roof of the smithy. It would be a long night.

* * *

In the bunkhouse, Elena sat and listened to her mother's distress.

'Elena, a lady never speaks her mind. You should be demure, feminine. Why, the Sanchez brothers would have been astounded at your words to those people outside the church.'

'She's got a little of her father in her,' Barker said, his eyes twinkling with pride.

125

'I'm sorry, Mother,' Elena said, 'but I was so angry. Not one of them was sorry about the house. Even the pastor seemed to think we were rightfully punished.'

'By the way,' her father said, 'there'll be no ridin' alone from now on.'

Elena sat down on her bunk and kicked off her satin shoes. It had been a tiring day. First, those indifferent people. Then that very pretty woman who gasped at seeing Ben. Lying back, still fully clothed, she tried to understand her own feelings. Ben had shot her brother, possibly in cold blood. But just being around him made her feel like a woman. No other man had ever been able to do that.

The gentlemen who flirted, the friendly cowhands, the Sanchez brothers — they were all distant faces. Ben was real.

'Elena, you're wrinkling your dress,' her mother said.

Sitting up, Elena began to fuss with the buttons and ribbons on her bodice.

Riding alone in the wind would help her think. Maybe she would do it tomorrow, while the men were getting ready for the roundup.

Someone would have to ride with her. She didn't want to disobey her father. Most of the men would be busy with the new broncs. She thought of Ben, then shook her head. No, it would be more prudent to take someone else.

★ ★ ★

After a poor night's sleep Elena awakened early. Her father was snoring loudly, her mother was sleeping fitfully. Elena smiled at them. They had had separate rooms because of his terrible snoring, but they loved each other very much.

She pulled on her new riding clothes, fretting over the wrinkles in the skirt. Her heavy wool coat, extending to her hips, would fight off the morning chill.

Outside, in the damp air, she saw the first light of sun over the Apache Rim, which circled most of the valley. She wanted to get up there and look down on the world. There were some trails on the east side of the valley that would take her up there, but she had her own secret way to the rim.

At the corral, she found two of the men taking a walk, and she asked them to get Jenson. Finding her sorrel mare among the standing but sleeping horses, she put a rope around its neck and led it outside the gate. She began to groom the animal lovingly.

Jenson soon appeared, sleepy but agreeable.

'My father won't let me ride alone,' she said. 'I want to go up the rim.'

'Them trails are mighty dangerous. And mighty far from here.'

'I know one that isn't.'

Reluctantly, he brought out a hammerhead roan and then saddled it and her mare. As they mounted, their Texas saddles creaked with their weight. His roan was chewing the bit and tossing its head, eager to take off.

They soon reached a high roll of hills. Elena reined up and turned in the saddle to look back. The ranch looked far away, forlorn, lonely.

There was a wind rising. The sun was warm, but clouds were moving in from the northwest. It could well rain before they returned. Elena didn't care.

She rode straight in the saddle, her long black hair flowing in the wind. Feeling grand and free, she urged her mare toward the foot of the great rim.

By early afternoon they were at the trail she had found. Her secret deer path, hidden in a crevice up the wall, was sheltered by huge rocks. She led the way up the north rim, their animals slipping and sliding in the soft dirt between the boulders. Jenson was amazed that the trail existed.

It was afternoon before their sweaty, panting animals brought them to the rim. They rode into the pine forest, then made their way around the patches of snow to the red rocks on the top of the rim. They dismounted, and loosened the cinches to rest their animals.

From here, they could see most of the valley, and it was a grand and glorious view. Jenson was nervous. He feared that Barker would have his hide. But he enjoyed the sight of this beautiful young woman sitting on the rocks with the green and crimson land spread below.

'I love this valley,' she said.

'Yes, ma'am, but if we're to get back afore dark, we'd best be goin'.'

She nodded, but she sat awhile longer, occasionally drawing a deep breath. The air was thinner up here. The crispness of the forest and the grand view were intoxicating.

Then she heard a new sound. A gasp. Turning quickly, she saw Jenson's wild face. He threw his hands in the air and staggered backward. He turned and fell facedown with a frantic cry. A knife was stuck in the center of his back.

Elena fought back a scream. She saw nothing but the forest behind them, but she sprang to her feet. Her rifle was in the saddle scabbard.

Face hot, body in shock but moving, she ran for her sorrel. The cinch was loose. It could be disaster to mount. She reached the animal and pulled out the rifle.

Before she could turn to take another look at the forest, she heard what could have been an animal sound. And then a big, ugly hand closed on her wrist.

7

The day had been spent with the green broncs. Every man who had tackled them was sore and dirty. They were fed over an open fire by old Carson, who did most of the cooking but not terribly well. Barker had promised them a real cook along with the new hands for roundup and the drive.

Ben had ridden a strong black he had liked. The animal had put up a dangerous fight, but Ben had stayed in the saddle. Sore all over, Ben had felt pretty good about it until Barker growled at him, 'Seems like you oughta be takin' better care of them hands.' Ben had only grinned back.

An hour before dark, Barker was pacing outside the bunkhouse like an animal caught in a trap. He kicked dirt while he gazed up at the partly cloudy sky. Elena had not returned with Jenson. His foreman came over to reassure him.

'They got to be all right,' Gridley said.

'Just the same, we can't wait any longer,' Barker told him. 'Get started lookin', in every blamed direction. Look at the river crossings.'

The weary men saddled and mounted. They spread out. Ben and two other men headed north toward the rim. There were a lot of tracks and hoofprints, but the herd had criss-crossed the hills. Nearing the great tide of beasts with their long horns and big bones, Ben reined up to look at them. He liked being around the herd. It made him feel like he was in Texas or on the trail to the railheads. It was a fine sight. The animals spread as far as the eye could see. There was a bounty of new calves, protected by angry cows.

But he couldn't enjoy what he saw. His mind was on Elena. He turned and caught up with the two men heading for the rim.

As night fell, they could still see. There was a full moon that even cast their shadows on the grass. The cattle were sprawled to the west of them, a great body of wiry, restless longhorns covering several knolls.

'No sign of 'em,' one cowhand said. 'You couldn't track a railroad train after them cattle been movin'.'

Clay could track it, Ben thought, and he wished his brother were here.

At the foot of the rim Ben reined up.

'There's got to be a trail up,' he said.

'Ain't none,' a man responded. 'Only east of here, across from where the fort is. Mighty long ride.'

'Then you fellas head that way, but keep checkin' the rim just the same. I'll ride west along it.'

The others rode off, following the rim in an easterly direction. Ben rode slowly back and forth along the face of the rim, moving west. His instinct told him that Elena would want to get

134

to the top for a view. She wouldn't have settled for less. He also felt that she would know this valley better than the men.

An hour later he saw a white-tailed deer scoot through the rocks along the foot of the rim. It knew where it was going.

Ben turned toward his last sight of it. It had taken a trail hidden by great red boulders. Ben rode to the site, between rocks. In the bright moonlight, he could see prints in the dirt, but they were so blown by the wind that he couldn't read them. The animal had disappeared.

It was possible that Elena had spotted the deer in the past on one of her rides. He would have to follow to get a better look. There was no use alerting anyone until he was sure of his hunch. He headed up the narrow trail, his mount responding with rippling muscles.

It took almost two hours in the dim light. Slowly but surely, his bay picked its way up the rise. No wonder the men didn't know about the trail. It had been hidden by the rocks below and was barely wide enough for one horse.

His bay strained the last few yards, fighting to reach the top, where it could finally rest. Ben directed their way into the great forest, where patches of snow gleamed in the moonlight.

He urged his horse through the trees and into the clear, riding toward the edge of the rim. There he dismounted. It was a natural place for a view.

But not for a man to die. Jenson lay facedown, a knife in his back.

Ben felt the hair on the back of his neck prickling. He looked around. There was no sign of life. Jenson's roan was gone. So were Elena and her sorrel mare.

He knelt and examined the hunting knife that could have been wielded by a white or a red man. Jenson had been dead since midafternoon, he decided, grimacing. He had liked the quiet cowhand.

Fury rose within him. Someone had taken Elena. The rim was so high that a rifle shot would not bring the cowhands. Worse, it would alert whoever had taken her.

Ben drew a deep breath. He needed all his skill just now. He had learned to be silent in the range wars as well as in the Army. He had fought Comanche and a few Apache, but it wouldn't be easy in a forest thick with underbrush.

He took the reins of his big bay, and walking ahead of the animal toward the forest, he looked for sign. There were tracks of three horses — Elena's, Jenson's, and the killer's. There was no sign of violent struggle, but the man must have grabbed her on the rocks near the edge of the rim.

Grim, determined, Ben was angry when the tracks disappeared onto the solid rock plateau that lined the top of the wall. But he wasn't going to give up the hunt. He couldn't turn back now. Come daylight, Gridley would be able to follow the hoofprints of Ben's bay.

He mounted and began to ride close to the forest, occasionally making a marker on a tree with his hunting knife. His rifle was in the scabbard, his Colts were at his side, and he was ready. He kept thinking of some savage putting his hands on Elena.

'I'm not afraid, now that you're here,' she had said at the hotel.

Memory of her courage on the trail drove him onward. It was the middle of the night when he saw the campfire deep in the forest, a small glow almost hidden by the pines.

He dismounted and ground-tied his bay. Slowly, as quietly as he could, he moved through the trees, trying to avoid the underbrush, fighting for rocks to step on, fearful that owls would scatter and announce his coming.

On his hands and knees, he completed the last hundred yards. What he saw astounded him, and yet he shouldn't have been surprised.

Elena was sitting cross-legged with

her hands tied behind her, facing in Ben's direction. She looked unharmed. A big man sat on Ben's side of the campfire. He was talking, and, immediately, Ben recognized Sid Holder's crackling tone:

'Then I got this here Apache, and I held him down and got his scalp. Yes, sir, I was pretty mad.'

Carefully, Ben moved closer.

'But that weren't nothin',' Sid Holder said. 'Why, I ran into this here grizzly up in the Shining Mountains. I'd been fishin' along a big creek and had a good pile of fish. Here comes the biggest bear you ever did see. Why, I grabs my Sharps and turns around and blasts him right between the eyes. Well, he keeps on acomin', and I pulls my knife and jumps back into the creek. But he's done for, all right.'

Ben would have been amused at all this except for Jenson's body and the way Elena was tied. Apparently, this was Holder's way of courting her.

Slowly, Ben got to his feet and began to walk normally, crackling the underbrush. Holder jumped up, spinning with his Winchester rifle in hand. He slapped a shell into the chamber and aimed at Ben. His ugly, bearded face was snarling.

Wanting to avoid a fight, Ben had not drawn his Colts, and his knife was tucked under his gun belt. Any violent action could harm Elena. Appearing calm and reasonable himself, he expected the blowhard to be the same, but he was prepared for the worst. He would try to talk the man down.

Elena's eyes grew round and fearful. Ben paused just within the light of the crackling fire. There was a long, tense silence. Then Holder laughed, still aiming his rifle at Ben, who kept his hands at his sides.

'Well, now,' Holder said, 'if it ain't the fast gun.'

'Untie her,' Ben told him, his voice even and cold.

'Get out of here. I aim to marry that woman.'

'You killed a man back there.'

'Prove it,' Holder said, moistening his lips.

'I'm going to have to take you in,' Ben said. 'I figure you'll be hanged for what you did.'

'Just doin' what any man woulda done for the likes of her. But right now, I got *you* on my mind, and I been think' how I heard you was claimin' you shot her brother while he had the drop on you. Well, I don't figure that ever happened. Maybe you better show me.'

'I got no mind to kill you,' Ben said.

'I'm gonna toss a bullet. When it hits the ground, you better draw or I'm puttin' lead in your gut.'

Ben didn't take his eyes off the man. His Colts weighed heavily at his sides. His gunfighting days had stopped one year ago, when he had been arrested. He was well aware that he was out of practice.

Holder's grimy hand tossed a bullet into the air. Ben watched it spin. As it fell and struck the ground, Ben's right hand flew up with a blazing Colt revolver.

As his shot struck Holder in the chest, the man fired, but the rifle bullet whistled by Ben's ear.

With his smoking six-gun in his hand, Ben watched the big man drop to his knees, a hand on his bloody chest. Amazement spread across the angry, bearded face. Then he crashed forward, facedown, and lay still.

Ben checked that Jenson's killer was dead. Then he holstered his gun and knelt at Elena's side. 'Is he the only one here?' he asked, cutting the ropes from her wrists.

'Yes,' she whispered.

'Are you all right?'

He sat back on his heels, looking at her face as she nodded and rubbed her hands. She was staring at him, and he felt mighty uncomfortable. He saw no gratitude, only a confused look. He stood up and drew a hand across his damp brow. Ben Darringer had added another notch to his gun. He didn't like it one bit. Holder had been more of a beast than a man, but it didn't set easy.

Infatuation may have driven Holder to take Elena, but cold brutality had caused him to knife Jenson in the back. The thought should have helped ease Ben's remorse, but it didn't.

'Where are the horses?' he asked.

She nodded toward the forest behind her. As she started to rise, he held out his right hand. Hesitantly, she slowly slid her small white fingers into his big rough ones. He pulled her to her feet, then let her hand slip away.

It would be daylight soon.

'What was he doin' up here?' Ben asked.

'The three of them were up here looking for mustangs. I think they have a camp some miles east of here. But he's the only one I saw. They'll be after you now.'

143

Ben shrugged, then dragged Holder's body into the trees. Then he knelt by the campfire, picked up the coffeepot, and poured some of the hot liquid into a tin cup.

'We have to get out of here,' she said.

He sipped the coffee. It felt good in his belly. She was impatient, but he was weary. Finally, she relented and sat down near the fire.

Then, a minute later, he was surprised when she rose, took an opened can of beans, and emptied it into the blackened frying pan. She shoved some pieces of bacon in with the beans, and placed the pan onto the rocks set in the flickering fire.

Recalling the long week from the steamer to the valley, and the way she had sat primly while Gridley prepared the food, he began to feel warm all over. She was doing it because he had saved her. She was thanking him in the only way she could.

'He wouldn't go to sleep,' she said.

'He was courting me by telling me of all the manly things he had done. He'd been talking for hours.'

'What I heard was mighty impressive.'

'It didn't compare to your facing his rifle.'

She didn't look at him as she said it. He knew it was the closest she could come to telling him that maybe he was as fast as he was reputed to be, and that, just possibly, he had not shot her brother in cold blood after all.

'You could have ambushed him,' she added.

She reached over to stir the beans. In another minute, she poured some into the tin plates and handed him one. They ate in silence. It tasted wonderful to Ben. Then she poured them more hot coffee.

Sitting back, she drew a deep breath, as if she had just realized that she was free from Holder. Then her eyes moistened as if she were going to cry.

'Poor Jenson,' she said.

'He never knew what hit him.'

'I know, but he was so young.'

'It's a tough land,' Ben reminded her.

She looked up through the trees, as if searching for daylight. Then he realized that, still thinking of Jenson, she was looking to heaven.

'It'll be light soon,' he said awkwardly.

Elena folded her arms, chilled even in her jacket. Ben wanted to take off his leather coat and put it around her. But he refrained. He was getting too close to her. The Barkers hated him. They also had his ticket to freedom.

'They say you've killed a dozen men,' she said.

'In the range wars there wasn't much choice. But I didn't go lookin' for your brother or this fellow Holder.'

They were both silent awhile, listening to the night sounds of the forest. Then she spoke quietly.

'You said you had three brothers. Are they like you?'

He shrugged. 'No. The next to the youngest — that's Clay — he wanted

146

to be a doctor. Then there's Hank, the toughest one of the bunch, probably wearin' a badge up in the Dakotas. And Jess, well, he's the youngest one, and plays the guitar. You met him down in Yuma. He's comin' with Shockley's herd.'

She gazed at him a long while, trying to connect him with his brothers, trying to understand this gunfighter.

'And your parents?' she asked.

'My father was killed by bandits before Jess was born. My mother's still down in Texas.'

'Do you miss her?'

Ben nodded.

She rose and stretched a little, aware that he was watching her. Soon they would be returning to the ranch, where her father would restrict her even more. There would be no more riding the wind on her sprightly mare.

Elena's grudge against Ben had been thrown into confusion. She had seen his miraculous speed with a gun. But she was afraid that her father would never believe her story. If she was to spend any time with Ben, it was now.

'But how is it you gave up the law to be a gunfighter?' she asked.

'Hank and Clay were in trouble. I helped them escape from jail so they wouldn't be hanged for somethin' they didn't do. After that, I didn't feel right about sitting down with a law book.'

'So what did you do?' she persisted.

'There was a range war brewin' more than one place in Texas and up north. Some over barbed wire. I got involved in a few. After that, in the fall of '75, I volunteered for ridin' with Captain McNelly's rangers, fighting border bandits and rustlers around Brownsville.'

'What made you head for Tucson?' she asked, referring to where he had killed her brother.

'McNelly gave me a good talking to,' Ben said. 'In early '76, I figured I'd find my brother Jess. He'd written me from Tucson. Thought we'd head for California, where maybe they hadn't heard of Ben Darringer.'

'But my brother had?'

'No disrespect, but he wasn't about to back off.'

'Rex was that way. He couldn't live up to being as tough as my father wanted. No matter what Rex did, my father could do it better. I think Rex developed a terrible need to prove himself.'

'What about you?' he asked.

'Oh, the usual finishing school for young women of our position. My mother wants me to marry some fine gentleman. We were in Kansas when we heard that her family was killed by Apaches, leaving her the land grant. We moved here in 1873. There were a lot of soldiers here then. General Crook had arranged peace with the Indians just before we arrived.'

'You seem to like it here.'

'I've never seen anything more beautiful. My father started the town, brought in people by wagon, and offered them lots to build on. He contracted with the Army to sell them cattle for the reservations. Because of the poor grass there, he didn't fight the small ranchers moving in south of the river. Now they've turned on us.'

'There's more to your father than meets the eye.'

'My father is worth more as a man than the whole lot of them who are fighting us. He's tough as a grizzly, but has a good heart. There's not a drop of mean blood in him.'

Their eyes met, and she smiled, a little embarrassed but still proud.

'Nearly light,' Ben said. 'I reckon we better get Holder onto a saddle.'

'You're taking him back?' she asked, a little surprised.

'Got to keep the story straight in town.'

He stood up and kicked dirt on the fire. Then she helped him bring the horses to the small clearing. As much as possible, she helped as he loaded Holder over the man's own saddle and then tied his arms to the stirrup leather on one side.

They led the horses through the thick forest, picking up Ben's mount, until they reached the open area near the rim's edge. There was no sign of any riders. They tightened cinches and swung into the saddle. Reining up, they looked down at the valley. They could see the herd, a great, sprawling shadow that covered several hills and disappeared beyond.

The sky was set with darkening clouds that were moving overhead from the north. The sun tried to shine through the trees. It was going to rain before they could get home.

They rode back over the rocky trail to where Jenson still lay. On a far rock, a black buzzard had just landed. Ben dismounted, picked up a stone, and cast it at the bird. It flapped its wings and took to the sky.

Shivering, Elena dismounted and helped Ben lift Jenson onto the hammer-head roan. The animal shuddered as the stiff body was draped across the saddle. Eyes burning, Ben tied the man into place, leaving the knife sticking out.

He turned to see tears in Elena's eyes.

'We got to show why Holder's dead,' he murmured.

She nodded, but she was shaking as she turned to remount.

Ben swung into the saddle. They rode side by side, each leading a burdened saddle horse.

Elena was sad, trying to forget Jenson, and she talked about her valley and how peaceful it had once been.

'It's not fair,' she said. 'The valley belongs to us. We're just waiting on word from Washington.'

'A lot of men are going to die before it comes.'

'What do you suggest? That we let our cattle go hungry while *their* herds take our grass?'

'No,' he said, shaking his head. 'But maybe you and your mother oughta be in town at the hotel.'

'I can use a rifle,' she said. 'And my mother has shot two Apache in her life. She would never leave my father.'

Ben thought of her demure, aristocratic mother in a new light, but it didn't change anything. It was dangerous for the women to be there.

When they reached the rocks that hid the trail, they paused to rest the horses. Ben leaned on the pommel, looking as far down as he could. The herd was spread in great waves across the northwest side of the valley. There were two riders with it. Beyond, he could see the river running east to west, glistening in the sunlight. It was a pretty sight.

The ranch buildings could barely be seen because of the rolling hills and clusters of aspen. There was a fuzzy line along the west river that was probably the town.

'It's beautiful,' Elena said.

'Someday I'll have a place like that.'

The words hung empty in the air. As empty as the dream.

He started through the rocks and down the narrow trail that was hardly a deer path. The bodies bounced off the boulders. It seemed forever before they found their way through the last barriers and onto the grassy flat.

As they stopped to rest the horses, he turned to her and said, 'We'll pick up a few hands and head for town. I don't want any trouble over this.'

The clouds were moving swiftly across the sky. They were already blocking out the sun. Elena looked intensely beautiful with her long black hair moving in the wind. Her dark blue eyes were suddenly cast aside in a new shyness.

They rode on, the wind tearing at them now. The sky was filling with dark clouds that covered the valley with speeding shadows. An hour later there was no blue sky left.

The rain began to fall, lightly at first, then vigorously, drumming them and the dry earth with great drops of water. It became so heavy that they hunched over in the saddle. Neither had a slicker. They were being soaked.

Off to the right, some of the herd were huddled under the few trees dotting the hills. The sky rumbled. On the far side of the valley, ribbons of light streaked down from the black clouds.

Elena shuddered. She looked frightened. Her mare was dancing and tossing its head.

'Let's ride,' Ben said.

They put the horses at a lope, the burdened mounts keeping pace. Hooves chopped at the wet grass and new mud. Powerful muscles rippled beneath their hides. Ben leaned forward, his hand on his bay's neck.

Lightning danced across a nearby knoll where three lone junipers sheltered a few head of cattle. He saw one of the animals jump and keel over on its side.

Suddenly he reined up. Stopping her sorrel, Elena turned in the saddle to look at him. The other horses nervously spun around behind them. Water was pouring off them.

'We can't outrun it,' he said. 'And we can't get near the trees. Is there a place where we can hole up?'

'There's a line shack,' she said.

She led the way along a gully. The rain was drenching them. Even his leather jacket couldn't protect his soaked Levi's. His legs felt like ice. Elena had to be in even worse condition.

Lightning slashed across the sky. The storm was raging, flooding the valley. Water was whirling down the gully around their horses' legs. They came to open ground where, in the far distance, he could see the shack. It was next to a creek, but there were no trees.

Two horses were tied up outside, the animals hanging their heads. Ben and Elena dismounted and tied the horses to the railing. They hurried to the door. Ben shoved it open, rain and wind sweeping in with them.

As they entered and slammed the

door behind them, they felt the heat of the stove. Sitting on the bunk, looking up in dismay and relief, was her father. Next to him was Gridley, wide-eyed.

Though she was soaked through, Elena ignored the stove and ran into her father's arms. He held her, his face pressed to her wet hair, tears in his eyes.

Looking away, Ben moved to the stove and warmed his hands. Gridley came over to him and asked, 'What happened?'

'Found her trail up to the rim. Jenson was knifed in the back. It was Sid Holder, taking her prisoner. To save her, I had to kill him. They're out on the horses.'

Barker listened carefully, still holding Elena tight.

'Couldn't have been easy,' Gridley said. 'Them Holders are mighty tough hombres.'

'We had to shoot it out,' Ben said, shrugging.

'No,' Elena said.

'What is it?' Barker asked her. 'What else happened up there?'

'I was sitting there all tied up,' Elena said, trembling. 'Sid Holder was trying to impress me by telling me about all his great adventures. He wasn't going to hurt me just yet, but I was afraid.'

'Then what happened?' her father prompted, glaring at Ben.

'It was all so unexpected. We heard a noise, and there was Ben. He had his guns in his holsters. He thought he could talk Sid out of a fight. So did I for a while.'

'Go on.'

'Sid had his rifle cocked and aimed at Ben. They kept talking. Then Sid started taunting him. Next thing I knew, Sid was throwing a bullet into the air. When it landed, he was going to kill Ben.'

Ben turned away, staring at his hands as he warmed them over the stove. Would she tell the truth? He could feel Barker's eyes burning through his back.

'It all happened so fast,' she said. 'The bullet hit the ground. Before Sid could pull the trigger, Ben had his six-gun out and was firing. He shot him dead, but it was self-defense.'

There was a long silence. Ben felt chilled, even near the stove. He could feel everyone watching him. The rain was drumming the roof; the wind was shaking the board walls. Thunder was rumbling through the sky.

'That sure enough true?' her father asked her.

'You that fast?' Gridley asked Ben.

Ben shrugged. 'He was overconfident.'

Elena came over to him and put a hand on his arm. He looked down at her lovely face. There was a new warmth in her eyes. It made him tremble down to his boots.

'Thank you,' she said. 'That's the second time you've saved my life.'

Barker cleared his throat. 'Well, listen, Darringer, I'm mighty grateful. No tellin' what them Holders would have done with my daughter. We oughta hunt down the other two.'

'No.' Elena turned back to her father. 'Ben wants to take the bodies to town and show the sheriff and everyone else that it was a fair fight. The knife is still in Jenson's back.'

'He's out there in the rain,' Ben said.

Gridley looked grim. He picked up a blanket and went outside. The wind and rain spun through the door until he closed it behind him.

Ben removed his jacket and hung it over a chair. He looked around the shack, which had several bunks and a lot of gear. It was warm despite the draft through some of the boards, and the shake roof was dry. There were four chairs and a small table.

Gridley returned, and after pouring water into a pot, he dumped in coffee grounds and set it on the stove. 'Maybe I oughta ride to the ranch,' he said to Elena. 'Your mother will be plenty worried.'

'I'll ride along,' Ben said.

Gridley pulled on his slicker. Ben reached for his jacket, but paused in surprise as Elena handed him her father's slicker. Barker said nothing. Ben pulled it on, grateful, and he followed Gridley out into the storm.

Standing by their horses, the cowhand turned to him and said, 'That was a fine thing you done, saving that child.'

Ben nodded. He felt better about it than he let on. The only time he had been this comfortable inside was after he had busted Clay and Hank out of jail.

They rode into the storm, leading the burdened horses.

★ ★ ★

Inside the shack, Elena shivered in her wet clothes as she spoke to her father.

'It was true,' she said. 'He drew faster than Sid could pull the trigger.'

'Don't mean that's how it was with your brother.'

'Think about it, Father. Rex was getting into a lot of trouble. He could have started some with Ben.'

'Listen to me, child. We want nothin' from this man but his gun. And you stay away from him. He ain't good enough for you.'

'He could have been a lawyer.'

'I got no use for them, either, so just forget about 'im.'

'I tell you, Father, when I was sitting there all tied up, I was awfully worried what Sid was going to do when he ran out of talk. When I looked up and saw Ben — Well, he was the answer to all my prayers.'

'You got no call to be more than grateful.'

She removed her wet jacket and stared at the coffeepot. Her father was probably right. A man like Ben was on the wrong road. Someday he would be shot down. But even now, she knew that she would cry for him.

8

When Ben and Gridley dismounted at the ranch, Elena's mother came running out of the bunkhouse with a cape over her head. Other hands rushed over to take the horses.

'Miss Elena's safe,' Gridley told her. 'Ben found her up on the rim. Sid Holder killed Jenson and kidnapped her, but Ben shot him. She's at the line shack with her pa.'

Relief flooded the woman's face. She hurried to Ben and, drawing herself up on her tiptoes, kissed his rough cheek. Then she turned and hurried back through the rain to the bunkhouse.

Ben couldn't move for a few moments. He could hear his heart pounding in his chest. Barker had thanked him. His wife had kissed him. Elena had looked at him with gratitude. Yet, he was still just a hired gun.

He followed Gridley to the smithy where they got into dry clothes. They were well fed that night, and Ben slept so soundly that he didn't awaken until Gridley shook him the next morning.

'Mr. Barker and his daughter came in early,' the cowhand said. 'The storm's over. We can go into town.'

After breakfast, a long procession started for town under a clear blue sky. In the lead were Barker and his daughter, riding side by side. Behind them rode Ben and Gridley. Next was a wagon carrying Jenson and Holder, driven by an old hand. The Sanchez brothers, packed and ready to take the boat to the Colorado, where they would take the steamer south, were next in line. Two young cowhands brought up the rear.

It seemed to take forever to get to the river, cross the high water, and head for town. Elena never looked back. She hadn't looked directly at Ben since thanking him in the line shack. All of a sudden she was shy, and he didn't understand it.

As they neared town, he thought of the letter in his pocket. He knew he had to see Caroline. Maybe he would believe her letter when he saw her.

The town soon came into view. The river seemed angry, flowing fast and swift, building height as it neared the boat ramp. Debris whipped at the banks.

Entering the muddy street, the procession slowed near the jail on the right. People came onto the boardwalks and stared. On the porch of the hotel, standing with other women, was Caroline.

The sheriff came out as Barker stopped his people.

'I want you to take a look under them blankets,' Barker said. 'Because I don't want no trouble from any of you.'

The round-faced lawman shrugged and lifted the blankets. The knife was still buried in Jenson's back. Barker gave the sheriff a complete account of what had happened, including Elena's story of how Ben had outdrawn a loaded rifle. Barker wanted word to get to Shockley, Ben was certain.

'Ain't no man that fast,' the sheriff grunted.

'You callin' my daughter a liar?' the rancher growled.

The sheriff shrugged, then shook his head.

Ben saw Clay standing behind some of the townsmen. He fought the urge to wave or grin. The look of pride on Clay's face gave Ben a mighty warm feeling.

'There's Walker,' Gridley said between his teeth. 'The one that looks like a hunk of wire in pants.'

Ben followed the cowhand's gaze to an ornery-looking cowman standing by a wagon up the street.

'I gotta get the Barkers out o' here before they see him,' Gridley muttered.

'All right,' the sheriff said to two husky men near him. 'Help me get 'em down and over to the barber's.'

Apparently, the barber was also the local undertaker.

As the wagons and riders turned to leave town, Ben held back, because he could see Caroline. Dressed in yellow and looking awfully pretty, she was waiting for him on the hotel porch. And he also wanted to see Clay.

'I'll catch up later,' he told Gridley.

Elena twisted in the saddle to look back at him.

Then a shot exploded in the air, singing past Ben's ear. Another shot blasted away as he turned in the saddle. Clay had fired at the hotel roof with his six-gun.

A man was standing on the eave of the roof, suspended in air, his rifle spinning downward. While a woman screamed, he came tumbling down like a sack of flour and crashed into the street near Caroline, who screamed and backed away. The old man's ugly face was turned skyward, eyes blank.

Ben's horse reared. He calmed it and dismounted.

A crowd slowly gathered around the body. It was Pa Holder, stone dead after seeking revenge for his son. Ben stood back near his horse, looking for Saul Holder. But there was no sign of him.

Clay was coming to his side, slowly holstering his gun.

'Good shot, Mr. Smith,' Ben said, his hand on Clay's shoulder. How he wanted to hug him.

'We're hirin' on,' Gridley told Clay as he rode over to them. 'We could use you. Right, Ben?'

'I'll think on it,' Clay responded.

Still mounted, Barker was shaking his head at the sight of the dead Holder. Elena looked drained.

Barker suddenly sighted Walker about to enter the saloon. He rode over to glare down at him. The wiry man glared back up with equal disdain.

'All right, Walker, we know it was your men who ambushed my daughter on the trail. What you got to say about it?'

'I didn't send 'em,' Walker said. 'When I come after you, it'll be wide open, and you can bet on that.'

'I'll be waitin',' Barker growled. Then he rejoined his daughter, who was moving away with the wagon and the dudes. Gridley followed with the other hands.

Only Ben remained. He heard a mumbling in the crowd about 'them Barkers, who bring nothing but trouble.' He watched the Sanchez brothers as they departed for the boat ramp, but not before each had kissed Elena's hand.

A heavy keel boat was coming upriver from the west, dragged along the bank by four mules led by a man. The boat was about twenty feet long and heavily loaded.

Ben looked at Clay, then shook his hand. 'There's another Holder still loose,' he warned.

'You hungry?'

'Sure. Why don't we eat at the hotel?'

'A little fancy for me. They got grub at the saloon. I notice you got a lady to see. Meet me over there when you're done.'

Ben had to grin. Clay never missed anything. In fact, he could have used him the day before. His brother could trail an Apache in the high rocks, and that took a lot of doing.

As Clay headed for the saloon, Ben walked around the men who were carrying Holder's body away. The other women on the hotel porch had gone inside. Caroline looked pretty in yellow, soft and appealing.

Ben stepped up onto the porch and walked toward her. Memories flooded and confused him. There had been sweet walks in the moonlight, hand-holding, kisses, promises. He had thought she was the sun, the moon, and the sky. Even now he felt a warmth rushing through him.

'Ben, did you get my letter?' she asked eagerly.

He nodded as he followed her to

the bench near the side of the hotel. No one else was around now. The crowd was gone. Barker's procession was nearly out of sight. Clay was back in the saloon.

And Ben was sitting next to Caroline. Her light blue eyes were glistening, her face was pink, and her yellow hair was done up in curls that fell to her soft throat.

'Ben,' she said, leaning toward him as much as she properly could, 'you look wonderful.'

'Your letter was a year late,' he said.

'Don't scold me, Ben. They wouldn't let me write.'

He swallowed hard. He knew now that he didn't want to hurt her. He still felt a lot of love for her. It confused him.

'All right,' he said with a shrug. 'You do look mighty fine. I reckon Rich Shockley agrees with me.'

'Ben, I never wanted to hurt you.'

He felt an urge to yell at her and punish her for desertion, real

171

or imagined. Instead, he could only see how pretty she was and remember what it was like to kiss her.

'Look, Caroline, I have to see this through, no matter what happens. I'll either earn a pardon with the help of the Barkers or I'll end up back in Yuma. You're better off marrying a man like Shockley, who can do right by you.'

She slid her hand toward his, then hesitated and withdrew it. Shielded from life, afraid to violate propriety, she was watching him with desperation in her eyes. He knew she wanted to be in his arms. Despite himself, he would have welcomed the chance to hold her.

'I've never loved anyone but you, Ben.'

He forced himself to stand. 'I have to go, Caroline. Clay Smith is waiting.'

'That awful man? He looks so terribly mean and unfriendly.'

'I reckon Shockley's herd will be showing up the other end of the valley right soon,' he said. 'But I don't figure on goin' to your wedding.'

'Oh, Ben! If only there was a way for us.' There were tears in her eyes.

Ben felt a tug at his heart. He turned and stepped back into the muddy street. He didn't look back, but he felt her tearful gaze following him. He knew he would have to see her again.

Crossing the street, he saw the Sanchez brothers boarding the keel boat, even as supplies were being unloaded. They were probably in a hurry to get back to their safe hacienda in Mexico.

He entered the noisy saloon where the piano player was singing 'I Ride an Old Paint.' The saloon woman was sitting with three men who looked like merchants. A drunk was asleep and snoring.

Ben joined Clay at the far corner table, and they sat with their backs to the wall and grinned at each other. The barkeep took their order for beef and beans, leaving them to pretend to play poker.

'You want to hire on?' Ben asked.

'Not right now. I figure I can do better for you if I'm just watchin'.'

'I wouldn't like it much if you got shot.'

Clay grunted. 'Neither would I.'

'Things are better with the Barkers,' Ben said. 'I think they have to believe I didn't murder their son.'

'If you believe that, you'll be settin' yourself up for disappointment, for one day you're a hero, and tomorrow you'll still be the man who robbed them of their son and brother.'

The barkeep brought their food and coffee, which was better than Carson's cooking. Ben thought of how Elena had cooked for him high up in the pines. Nothing would ever taste that good again.

'So that was Caroline,' Clay said.

'Yes. I don't rightly know what to do about it.'

'Don't be too hard on her. Most women do what their families say. That Elena Barker, she'll be marrying some

174

dude that her mother picks out. And you can bet on that.'

They had their meal and talked about Texas and their brothers. Clay remembered most of their mother's discipline. They talked of how their father had been murdered by bandits before Jess, the youngest, was born. Mostly, they remembered Texas.

Ben told Clay about his adventures with the Rangers. He added that he had then gone to Tucson to meet Jess, only to get mixed up with Caroline and with Elena's brother.

The day was wearing on, and Ben knew that he had to get back. It was obvious that Clay was concerned about him.

'I got you into this, Ben, and I ain't feelin' too good about it. I've seen this Zevala. He's cold, clean through. A man like that don't know how to be afraid. That makes him mighty dangerous.'

'Well, I know what it's like to be afraid. In the trenches during the war.

Standing in front of Holder's rifle. Sitting there with Caroline just now.'

'No Darringer is ever afraid. Just mighty cautious.'

Ben grinned, grateful for his brother's being here.

They parted reluctantly. In the street, Ben paused and looked toward the hotel. A year ago he had loved that woman with all his heart. Now he wasn't sure.

He mounted his bay and rode out of town along the raging river. He wondered behind which bush or tree Saul Holder might be hiding, waiting to shoot him down.

Toward evening he fought his way back across the river and then passed the two riders standing guard. Riding over the knolls that gave him a view of the ranch, he had a feeling there would be no roundup. Instead, the valley was going to break loose with one devil of a war. There would be stampedes, fighting, and killing. But first, there would be Zevala.

Some of the men were in the corrals, still trying to break a couple of the broncs that the Holders hadn't spent much time with. Ben paused at the fence and watched two men holding a horse by the ears, its eyes covered with a sack. One of the young cowhands eased into the saddle on its back.

Then there was an explosion as the animal reached for the sky, behaving like an angry grizzly. Ben stood back as the rider came reeling over the top board, almost into his arms, and then hitting the ground with a thud.

Young Peters rolled over and sat up, looking stunned. Then his freckled face broke into a grin.

'Let me at 'im,' Peters said. He staggered to his feet and climbed back over the fence.

Ben smiled as he walked away, remembering his early days in the saddle. He walked past old Carson, the grubby hand, who was stirring some kind of stew over an open fire. It didn't smell too wonderful.

Looking toward the bunkhouse, Ben saw no sign of the Barkers. Up on the knoll, the remains of the great old house were marked by the stone chimney. It looked forlorn.

At the smithy shed, he found Gridley soaping his saddle. Ben sat down, weary.

'Been a long day, has it?' Gridley asked.

'I don't much like bein' shot at.'

'That Clay Smith sure saved your hide. Good man.'

Ben took off his hat and wiped his brow as Gridley continued talking:

'That old man musta been mighty mad to shoot at you right in town when he didn't have much chance to get away. I reckon Saul Holder's still around somewhere, bein' a mite more careful. The boys are watchin' for 'im.'

'He'll show,' Ben said.

'And we just got word that Shockley's herd is in the valley, headin' for the fort and his spread.'

Ben leaned back on a stack of wood. He gnashed his teeth as he thought of the days ahead.

★ ★ ★

In the next few days, Ben saw little of the Barkers. He and the men were getting the mustangs and gear ready for the roundup. The herd was scattered all through the valley on the north side of the river. There was some brush country across from the fort and Shockley's spread, and a lot of cattle had disappeared up there, looking for shelter during the storm.

There would be a lot of riding, roping, and branding. A man could feel good about that, sweating in the sun, his muscles aching by the end of day. Ben looked forward to it.

But on Saturday, two men on horseback were escorted by one of the Barker men all the way from the river to the bunkhouse area. Most of the other Barker men were either out riding or heading to town. Ben and Gridley were at the corral with Peters and Carson. All but Ben retrieved their rifles. He was wearing his Colts. They turned to watch the two strangers. Barker and Elena came out of the bunkhouse.

The two men wore chaps and hats with chin straps. They had been on the trail a long time. One was young and arrogant, his peach-colored face frozen into a sneer. He wore a tied-down six-gun and carried a rifle. The other man was Jess, looking relaxed but tired.

Ben fought the urge to call out and show recognition.

'My name's Jess Darringer,' his brother said.

Barker looked startled. Ben walked forward slowly.

'That's far enough,' the arrogant one said. 'I'm the Texas Kid. Maybe you've heard of me.'

'Not likely,' Ben said.

'Mr. Shockley sent us,' Jess said. 'He'd like a powwow with Mr. Barker.'

'Let him come here, then,' Barker said.

'He don't figure it's safe,' the Texas Kid snapped.

Ben already disliked the man intensely. Gridley, rifle leveled at his hip, was grimacing. As old as he was, Carson looked ready to fight. Young Peters wasn't sure.

'We'll meet him in town,' Ben said. 'At church.'

The Kid laughed suddenly. He jerked at his horse's mouth and spun it around cruelly. Starting back toward the river, he reined up when he realized that Jess wasn't following.

'I want to talk with my brother,' Jess said.

'It ain't right,' the Kid snapped.

'Get along. I'll catch up.'

For a long moment, the young gunman hesitated, but he knew that he was outnumbered. Grimly, he turned and rode onward, escorted by the Barker rider.

Carson and Peters turned back to

the corral. Gridley went over to the far sheds. The Barkers stood in front of the bunkhouse for a while. Then, while Barker went back inside, Elena stood gazing at Jess and Ben. Then she walked over to them.

As he dismounted, Jess was appreciating the stunning beauty that had been hidden behind the veil at Yuma. Ben was uncomfortable. He still saw that same shyness in her glance. It was as if she had never held a rifle or ridden a bronc, as if she were helpless and demure.

'Miss Elena,' Ben said, 'do you remember my brother Jess?'

Gallantly, Jess took her outstretched hand, bowed, and kissed her fingers. Ben was surprised. Elena was pleased.

'Would you work for us, Jess?' she asked.

'Not right now, ma'am.'

'Have you seen this Zevala?'

Jess nodded. 'Now, there's a man who sends cold shivers down your back. He don't take to anyone. He just rides and sits and smokes and looks mean.'

Elena looked at Ben. He saw fear in her eyes. She seemed full of things to say, but she only shook her head. Sadly, she turned away.

They watched until she was back inside the bunkhouse.

'Say, Ben, is she worried about the ranch or you?'

'I'm through tryin' to figure out women.'

'Did you see Caroline? I reckon she'll remember me all right. She thought I was a bad influence on you. Good thing she never met Clay or Hank.'

They walked together as Ben told him about Caroline and Clay. He also told him about the Holders. Jess told about the rough week's drive he had shared with Shockley.

'This Rich Shockley pretends to be a nice, clean boy, but I seen him torture a rabbit before killin' it. You don't want to turn your back on him.'

'How about old man Shockley?'

'A real rattlesnake, but a good hand. He wants this valley, that's for sure. He don't care about Walker, but he's already meetin' with him and some of the small ranchers.'

'How many men does Shockley have?'

'Thirty with the herd,' Jess said. 'Plus me and Zevala and that Texas Kid, who's spoiling for a fight. And any of the small ranchers who might join in.'

'Why do you figure he wants to meet with Barker?'

'When the killin' starts, Shockley doesn't want any problems with the law. He figures that if he shows an effort to take the grass peaceably, no one can blame him when there's a fight.'

'And I guess there's going to be a fight,' Ben said.

'A real range war. Shockley ain't bashful.'

'How do you figure he'll come at us?'

'I don't know, but it could be wide open and full blast.'

'We'll be hirin' on another dozen men in another week for the roundup. Even then, sounds like we'll be outnumbered.'

'After the powwow,' Jess said, 'I figure that Zevala's going to call you out, right in the middle of town. If you can take Zevala, it'll slow Shockley down some, cool things off, maybe.'

'What about you, Jess? If you ride back to Shockley's, the Texas Kid will already have you in trouble for talking to me.'

'Don't worry none about that. I told Shockley that I'd be talkin' to you. He thinks I'm recruitin' you to come over to his side. I'll have to tell him you turned me down.'

They walked together a while. Then Jess returned to mount his buckskin gelding. He leaned on the pommel, talking low to Ben.

'I tell you one thing, Ben. That Elena has got to be the most beautiful woman on earth. And if you're thinkin' too much about her, it could get you in a lot of trouble.'

'She's too much for any man. All I want is my freedom.'

'Well, I'll be ridin' on. See you in church.'

Ben watched his brother ride south, then turn to wave. Ben lifted his hand in farewell. He was mighty fond of his three brothers, but Jess had something extra special — a gentle heart.

Ben turned back toward the corrals. He knew full well that, tomorrow morning, church was not going to be followed by a picnic.

9

Sunday morning, dressed in their fine clothes, the Barkers took the wagon and headed for town. In the lead rode Gridley, Peters, and Carson. In the rear, Ben rode alone, his mind churning.

Clay was in town. Jess was with Shockley. Elena was acting strange. Caroline was waiting for him to make a move. Saul Holder was out there somewhere, plotting ambush. Zevala and Shockley were on their way.

It was a beautiful valley. But it would be an ugly war. There was no sign of the enemy. They had to be riding a southerly trail, avoiding the main road and the Barkers. The sun was warm, the ground fairly dry. The river had receded. The crossing was rough, but they made it without roping together.

Barker had given Ben no instructions.

He would have to play it by ear and wait and see what moves were made.

When they reached town, there was no sign of Shockley, Zevala, or the small ranchers. People stood on the street and watched the parade of Barkers.

On the hill by the church, pulling up among the other wagons, Barker halted his team. Then he jumped down and helped the women to the ground.

Singing came from inside the building. Ben looked back toward town. It was going to be a long day.

Gridley and the other two men took care of the horses and remained near the wagon, waiting and watching.

Ben followed the Barkers inside, where they again took the rear pew to the right. Ben sat on the edge of the empty pew to the left. The singing and music stopped, and the pastor scanned the church with his small eyes.

'I still see avarice in this room,' he roared. 'I see trouble. Men against men. Women weeping. I tell you, brethren, there's going to be a war in this valley.'

Ben glanced at the Barkers. The old man looked grim, but he wasn't going to stand up and say he'd give away his land to keep the peace. Ben couldn't see Elena's face. He did see Caroline up front, her hair prettied up with ribbons. Next to her was a man in a dark suit. He sat very close.

Ben's mouth was dry. He didn't want to listen to the sermon any longer. He stood up and went out the open door to breathe some fresh air. Walking over to the men, he looked at them inquiringly.

'No sign of 'em,' Gridley said.

'Rich Shockley's in there with his lady,' Ben told him.

'You figure he won't make trouble now?'

'Maybe in town, but keep your eyes open.'

The morning dragged. Ben returned to the church. He listened to the hymn, mouthing the words, and looked out

189

the door from time to time.

When the service was over, he went out before the pastor came forward. Standing with Gridley and the men, he saw the Barkers exit and cordially greet the pastor. Other people filed out, avoiding the Barkers, who soon headed for the wagon.

Then he saw Caroline, her arm through that of a lean, pleasant-looking young man, his face all smooth but for a tiny mustache. Ben felt a wave of jealousy, but he reminded himself that he was supposed to be angry at her.

Caroline chatted with the pastor while her escort walked over to the Barkers. Ben stood near the front wheel of the wagon, sizing up the man. He was in a Sunday suit, unarmed. There was no obvious sign that this man was the type to torture a rabbit. That made him dangerous.

'Mr. Barker? I'm Rich Shockley. My father spent the night in the hotel. He'd take it kindly if you'd meet him in the lobby.'

Sitting on the wagon seat next to the ladies, Barker glared down at him, but he nodded finally.

'Thank you,' Rich Shockley said. 'I'll let him know you're comin'.'

As Rich headed back toward Caroline, she glanced stealthily at Ben. She took Rich's arm, and they strolled over to a buggy where he carefully helped her aboard.

Ben tore his gaze away and turned to the Barkers. 'You want us at the meeting?' he asked.

'Just you and Gridley,' the old man said.

Ben and the others mounted, and they all moved down the hill into the Sabbath-still town. At the hotel, they tied up near Shockley's buggy.

Barker ordered the two women to the restaurant in the hotel. Then he, Gridley, and Ben followed them only as far as the lobby, while the others waited outside.

Sitting in soft chairs in the empty lobby, the three men waited. Barker looked mean but concerned. Gridley looked as if he were falling asleep.

'If we don't stop this war,' the rancher said, 'we'll lose everything. But I ain't turnin' my land over to the likes of them.'

'We got another dozen men coming,' Gridley said. 'But Shockley has thirty hands plus three guns and the other ranchers. Won't be easy defendin' open country.'

Barker turned to Ben. 'What's your brother doin' ridin' for Shockley?'

'Don't worry about Jess. He's a good man.'

Barker studied Ben for a long while. Then he said, 'I know you're only in this for that pardon, but you got to know you're likely to get killed. You want to face Zevala? Or you want to ride out? I won't stop you, not after what you did for Elena.'

'Ride out?' Ben asked, surprised.

'Right now, if you've a mind to.'

'I can't do that, Mr. Barker. Besides, I deserve that pardon.'

The old man considered what to reply. Finally he just shrugged. They fell silent, each measuring the other. Then they saw two men coming down the stairs — Rich Shockley in his Sunday suit and a wiry old man with a crooked nose and handlebar mustache. He wore trail clothes and a sidearm.

The Shockleys sat down on the couch across from Ben, Gridley and Barker. There was no one else in the lobby, either out of courtesy or fear.

The two old men glared at each other while trying to be civil.

'This is my father,' Rich said. 'Lane Shockley. Dad, this is Jack Barker.'

'That's my foreman, Gridley,' Barker said. 'And this here's Ben Darringer.'

Ben studied Rich Shockley while he thought of him with Caroline. He didn't like it one bit.

The older Shockley set his gaze square on Ben, sizing him up and sneering a little at the twin Colts. This was a tough old Texan who didn't set much store by a fast gun.

Ben could see that. He probably had just as little respect for Zevala, Jess, and the Texas Kid.

'Now look here, Barker,' Lane Shockley said, 'you're tryin' to hold on to government range. We got just as much right to that grass as you have. The railroad's gonna be comin' through in a couple of years. There's copper on the south mountain. This valley is going to boom, and you know it.'

'I own the valley, and I don't care if the railroad comes through,' Barker said. 'I figure it's just as well to herd the cattle to the nearest railhead or sell 'em to the Army.'

'Listen, Barker, if it weren't me, it'd be someone else movin' in, and I'm more reasonable than most.'

'So am I,' Barker said, 'as long as you don't try crossin' the river.'

The two men glared at each other, taking measure.

Rich cleared his throat. 'Look, Dad, maybe you and Mr. Barker could work out some kind of partnership.'

'What's he got to offer?' Barker snapped.

'Well, for one thing,' Lane Shockley said, 'I got me one handsome and educated son. You got an unmarried daughter. Maybe we're goin' about this all wrong.'

'Your son's already matched up,' Barker growled.

'Don't worry about that,' Rich said. 'Fact is, I saw your daughter, Mr. Barker. I'd be right on her doorstep if I had the chance.'

'You don't have much loyalty,' Barker observed.

'We're still talkin' partners,' Shockley said. 'What about it?'

'No.' Barker shook his head. 'Now what else you wanta talk about?'

'Back to the grass,' Shockley said. 'As soon as my herd's in position, we're crossin' the river.'

'We have a Spanish land grant,' Barker snapped. 'Pretty soon the word will come from Washington that it's authentic and legal. You want your men to die for nothin'? They'd be easy pickin's, trying to cross over.'

'We can ford near the Army post,' Shockley pointed out, not giving an inch. 'Unless your fancy gun here can stop us.'

'I hear you got one of your own,' Barker said. 'At least my man has some decency. You had to bring Zevala.'

'We're not getting anywhere,' Rich said.

He and his father stood up and walked around the couch.

Shockley paused, then gave Barker a grim sneer. 'You asked for it, Barker.'

Ben watched the Shockleys go back up the stairs. If they intended to start trouble today, they would be getting word to Zevala. Ben felt mighty cold inside.

'Let's go,' Barker said, getting to his feet.

Ben stood up, grateful that the old man thought he had some decency in him. That was worth almost as much as the pardon.

People had disappeared from the streets. The sheriff had also found somewhere else to be. Most of the horses had been removed from in front of the saloon across the road. There was the stillness of before a gunfight or larger battle.

Barker and Gridley stayed on the porch near the door. They sensed the same action Ben did. Slowly, Ben walked to the edge of the porch and looked up and down the street. He saw faces at windows, peering out fearfully.

He had examined his guns before church. He was conscious of their weight in his holsters. This was a day that would determine if Ben Darringer lived or died.

No one had ever taken Zevala, who killed without remorse, like an animal. Ben had no urge to fight, but he wasn't going to turn tail and run.

There was a long, deadly silence in the town. He could hear the distant roar of the river, the pounding of his own Texas heart.

Turning toward the livery, he saw a shadow. And then a man appeared on the street. He had silver conchos on his black hat and his gun belt. He was dressed in black, with a black leather vest. His arms were long at his sides. His fingers dangled near his holsters.

It had to be Zevala, his cruel face shaded from the sun. He had a square jaw, high cheekbones, an ugly, wide mouth that twisted down at the corners. He was clean-shaven, and looked like the picture of Death itself.

Ben stepped down into the dirt and walked slowly toward the center of the street. The sun was almost in his eyes. He couldn't change that. He stood quietly, his hands at his side, flexing his fingers.

Zevala was walking toward him. They were a hundred feet apart. Ben felt sweat on his body. He had never faced a more formidable foe. Now they were fifty feet apart. Thirty feet apart.

At twenty paces, Zevala slowly hooked

his thumbs in his gun belt, but he kept walking.

There was not going to be a fight, Ben realized. The man continued until he was about five feet from Ben, and then stopped there to face him.

They studied each other in silence. Zevala looked as mean as sin. His eyes were black and gleaming under heavy brows. He smelled of soap and tobacco. This was a man who could kill a man as easily as he could stomp on a spider, with as little regret.

'Just wanted to take your measure,' Zevala said, his voice thick with a Spanish accent.

'You're big on show.'

'For a man like me, it is important.'

'I suppose it raises the price,' Ben said.

'Do not sweat, my friend. I never kill a man on Sunday.'

'That don't stop me,' a voice called out from the alley next to the hotel, behind Zevala.

They carefully turned their attention

on the man who was walking into the street. It was the Texas Kid, his round, peach-colored face a bit redder, his blue eyes narrowed. His little mouth was twisted in a snarl.

Zevala merely smiled, an evil, sinister smile. He turned his back on the Kid, taking another long look at Ben Darringer. Then he turned and walked toward the saloon.

Ben was left standing in the street, facing the Texas Kid. The man was in his mid-twenties, his hard body standing as tall as possible.

Ben had no hunger to kill him. Also, it would be embarrassing to die at the hand of this arrogant gunman.

'Ben Darringer,' the Kid said, spitting the name from his lips. 'You don't look so tough.'

'Why don't you just back off?' Ben growled.

The Kid looked toward Zevala, who had stopped in front of the saloon. He was showing off for the supreme killer. He was also giving Zevala a chance to see how fast Ben was. It would give Zevala an edge when their time came.

'I'm going to kill you,' the Kid said.

They were both conscious of all the faces in the windows, of Zevala, of Barker on the porch. About sixty feet apart, they had to be closer for a good shot. The Kid began to move, cautiously but surely, toward Ben. He stopped at twenty feet, his hands clenching and unclenching at his sides.

'Go ahead,' the Kid sneered. 'Let's see how fast you really are.'

'I got no reason to draw on you.'

'Then I'll give you a reason,' the Kid said, reaching in his vest pocket. 'When this gold piece hits the dirt, you'd better draw or you'll be dead.'

Ben remembered Sid Holder's pulling the same stunt, but the Kid's highly toned reflexes would be a lot faster than Holder's rifle.

The coin went spinning into the air.

Ben felt his insides wrench. His face was damp. He heard the town holding its breath. The sun seemed brighter suddenly.

The coin hit the dirt.

Ben's gun flew into his right hand, spitting fire as the Kid's gun barely cleared the holster. The bullet struck midchest, and the Kid staggered back, firing.

Ben felt a thud in his left arm near the shoulder. As the pain shot through him, he reeled backward a step, the hammer on his six-gun already drawn back.

The Kid dropped to his knees and started at Ben. Then he clutched his chest and fell backward. The barber appeared and knelt beside the Kid. He probed here and there, then shook his head.

Ben was shaken. He didn't like this one bit. And he was hurt. This was the first time he had been hit in a gunfight. He had always been so fast that his opponents lost their momentum. But the Kid had thrown a lucky shot.

Always prepared, the barber came over to Ben and cut his shirt with a pair of scissors.

'Well, you was lucky,' the little man said. 'Went clean through. Come on over and I'll fix you up.'

Ben looked at Zevala. The man was just watching, a little amused perhaps. People began to come out of the buildings. Then he saw Clay on the boardwalk, even as Zevala disappeared into the saloon. There was no sign of the sheriff.

About to follow the barber, Ben paused and looked up at his employer. Standing with arms folded, Barker nodded approval. In the doorway of the hotel stood Elena. At her side, pushing out from the crowd, was Caroline. Both women looked stricken.

Ben followed the barber into his shop, set between the livery and the hotel. The barber sat him down in the high chair after removing his jacket and shirt. The skin was sliced right next to where the bullet had hit him during the canyon fight en route to the valley. The other wound had already healed.

After his arm was patched up, Ben learned that he owed the man two dollars. The white bandage on his arm was already spotted with blood, but the barber assured him that the bleeding would stop in a half hour.

There was a knock on the back door of the shop. With an odd look, the barber went to see who it was. He returned with Caroline, her face devoid of color. The barber took the hint and went out the front door, closing it behind him.

Ben stood up, uncomfortable that she was there.

'I took a terrible chance,' she whispered.

'Caroline, I'm all right.'

'I was so frightened.'

Suddenly, she rushed into his arms. Unprepared, confused, he held her as she stood on tip-toe and kissed him squarely on the lips. It brought memories roaring back like a steam engine, deafening him, sending shivers down his spine.

As she drew back, she smiled at him.

'I wanted to do that when I first saw you at the church. Oh, Ben! What can we do about us?'

'I don't know,' he said, releasing her.

She clasped her hands to her heart. 'If only my family would understand.'

'Does it really matter what your family thinks?'

'Why, yes, Ben, you know it does.'

'So if I got a pardon, they wouldn't mind your marrying an ex-gunfighter.'

'But you'd go back to studying law, Ben. You'd be somebody.'

'That's important to you, isn't it?'

'It would please my family,' she said.

He studied her, trying to remember. Yes, she had told her family again and again that he was going to be a lawyer. They had even talked about helping him find an office. Lawyers often became politicians. He had been acceptable then.

'I'd better go,' she said, uneasy. 'Rich would be terribly angry if he knew I was here. He has no idea that I knew you before, that I love you.'

She retreated toward the back room, looking pretty with her yellow hair and soft blue eyes. He still loved her. He knew that now. But it was all wrong.

Blowing him a kiss, she turned and hurried through the other room. He heard the back door closing. He drew a deep breath, then turned as he heard voices at the front door.

'I told you,' the barber was saying, loudly. 'My patient is resting.'

The door burst open. It was Barker, with Elena behind him.

'Well, now,' the rancher said, 'you don't look so all-fired hurt. My daughter insisted you were dyin'.'

'He can go,' the barber grunted.

Elena's face was flushed, and she wouldn't meet Ben's gaze. The three of them walked past the barber into the sunlight. It was time to go home.

When they were all mounted and the Barkers were in the wagon, Ben looked across the street. Standing side by side on the sidewalk, watching them, were Zevala and Clay.

It was an odd sight. Ben suddenly began to worry. Surely Clay wouldn't take on Zevala just to keep Ben from fighting him.

'I'll catch up,' he told Barker.

As the wagon and horsemen rode away, Ben turned his mount to cross the street. He reined up, then looked down at Zevala and Clay.

'Now I know,' Zevala said.

The killer smiled and went back into the saloon. Clay walked over to Ben's horse.

'Look,' Ben said, 'you stay away from Zevala.'

'Don't worry, big brother. Besides, I've decided to hire on with you. You need protection.'

Ben grinned as he leaned on the

pommel. 'When?'

'Soon's I saddle up. Be back in a minute.'

Clay's mount was a big black. The two brothers left town and set their horses at a gallop. When they caught sight of the wagon along the river, they slowed to a walk. It was like the old days, brothers against the world.

★ ★ ★

Elena turned on the wagon seat, curious about the strange man riding with Ben.

'Zevala is going to kill that boy,' her mother said. 'Jack, isn't there anything you can do?'

Barker shrugged. 'Not likely.'

'There's going to be a terrible fight.'

'That's why I sure wish you women would stay in town.'

'What about the Federal marshal?' Elena asked.

'It's been a long time since we sent for 'im,' her father said. 'Don't look like he's comin'.'

The Barkers fell silent. They knew that they couldn't give up the land that was theirs. Yet, because of this, a lot of men were going to die.

Elena looked back at Ben. Her mother tugged at her sleeve, but Elena couldn't take her eyes from Ben. He was such a strange man, a mystery. And he was going to die.

Again her mother tugged at her sleeve.

Slowly, Elena turned to look forward. Tears were in her eyes.

10

Sunday night at the ranch, Clay had been welcomed as a Darringer. He was wanted in Texas, not Arizona, and he was tired of being Smith. He joined Ben and Gridley in the shelter of the smithy. It was cold, with a bright moon and a lot of stars. A fire was blazing in the iron pit. The wind had died down.

'Maybe I oughta go talk with them Army boys at the post,' Clay said.

'We tried that,' Gridley responded, stretching out with his head on his saddle. 'Only a handful of men there. The rest are down south huntin' Apaches.'

'So in a few days,' Clay said, 'you get another dozen hands that aren't bargaining for a fight. How's that crazy old man think he's going to keep Shockley and the others from crossing?'

'Well, there are only two places where you can ford — where you crossed tonight and down by the post. We got men guardin' both.'

'But you're talking about cattle,' Ben pointed out. 'I figure there are several places a man on a good horse could cross.'

'I know. Come sunup,' Gridley said, 'we'd better do some scoutin'.'

'Clay here is the best tracker west of the Mississippi,' Ben told him.

Clay seemed embarrassed. They settled down for the night. Ben felt good, having his brother sleeping near him. He lay back, listening to the other men snore as he thought of Caroline. She had certainly surprised him at the barber's.

Restless, continually waking up, he slid out of his blankets, dressed, and left the shelter. He could see a man sitting his horse on the south knoll. Everything seemed peaceful.

And yet he felt the hairs standing up on the back of his neck. Something was wrong. He looked toward the bunkhouse where a soft light was still aglow. He saw a figure moving in the shadows near it.

Six-gun springing into his hand, he hurried across, the moon casting his shadow before him. He came up behind the skulker as he walked around the building, and he shoved his gun in his back.

'Reach,' Ben said grimly.

The man held up his hands and turned, backing into the moonlight. Ben was startled to see Jack Barker, who lowered his hands as Ben holstered his gun.

'You feel it too,' Barker said. 'Somethin's wrong.'

'Except we still got that man on the south knoll.'

'He can't see the river from there. If they got our boys, they could be crossin' now.'

'More likely they'd try it at the post,' Ben said. 'I'll take a look.'

'I'll go with you.'

'No, you'd best stay with the women. I'll take Clay.'

Back at the smithy, Ben shook Clay awake. Within minutes, they had mounted and were riding south with Winchesters in hand.

At the knoll, they found Peters on guard. He hadn't seen or heard anything. At the river, the two men were all right and having a smoke under the aspens.

'It's got to be the post crossing,' Ben said.

Together in the moonlight, they rode inland and then south. The only sound was the distant roar of the river and the thud of their horses' hooves.

By the time they neared the river crossing close to the fort, it was nearly dawn.

As they reined up in a grove of aspen, they could see smoke curling up from the distant post with its timber walls, set southeast of the river. There were scattered outbuildings. Only a few windows were lit.

The crossing was in view down below, but they saw no sign of man or beast. The Barker riders had disappeared.

'I don't like the smell of it,' Clay said.

Slowly they ventured forth. They sensed death in the air, but saw no bodies. No stray horses could be seen, either.

First light cast shadows from the rim. Ben and Clay rode up to the crossing. Tracks led from the river and north to the hills.

Clay dismounted and walked a few yards. 'At least forty horses,' he said. 'No cattle.'

Ben grimaced at the silent hills. It was a big valley, but Clay could track them anywhere. Yet Ben hesitated. He felt cold all over. Something was mighty wrong.

'Clay, we'd better get back to the ranch.'

'I figure you're short two men already.'

They set back along the river at a lope, pacing their horses as best they could. It was a long way back. And it was light already.

'You think he's after the herd or the ranch?' Clay asked.

'The ranch. It's wide open there.'

There would be no cover except from the buildings. A surprise attack could cut the defenses in half. Ben hoped that Barker was still wandering around outside.

They had to stop and walk their horses awhile, because the animals were panting and sweating. Time was passing. Anything could be happening at the ranch. Soon they set their mounts into another lope, straining the great hearts.

As they neared the ranch area, they heard gunfire. And on the next knoll, they could see the attack. At least forty riders, firing rapidly, were circling the corrals and buildings. Flashes of gunpowder came from the bunkhouse and the smithy. The other sheds were silent, and their front doors were open.

Ben and Clay forced themselves to rest their horses a minute. The animals were breathing hard. Finally, they could wait no longer and charged toward the battle. They both let out a rebel yell.

Ben took the reins in his teeth, ignoring the rifle in his scabbard, holding both six-guns as he neared the raging torrent of men. Clay had a rifle in one hand, a six-gun in the other, and reins in his teeth. They were a two-man army, charging forth to victory or death.

Smoke poured from the roof of the bunkhouse. It had been fired. In the whirl of fury, Ben saw Shockley and his son, both riding and shooting among their horde. The ground was strewn with the bodies of men who had ventured from the sheds.

Ben and Clay knew that they had to get the men who paid the wages. By instinct, they separated.

Nearly thirty of the attackers were still in the saddle. One yelled and whirled his mount as he saw the brothers barreling toward them.

'Hey, boss!' the man yelled.

Lane Shockley spun his horse about and fired at Clay, who was almost upon him. Clay's bullet hit the man in the shoulder, knocking him from the saddle.

Rich Shockley shrieked and came at them, shooting.

Ben fired and hit him in the neck. Rich gasped, grabbed his throat, and tried to turn his horse. The animal jumped and Rich plummeted to the ground.

As the other riders grouped for a charge on the brothers, gunfire from the smithy and bunkhouse hit them hard because they weren't moving. Ben and Clay also turned their attention on them, firing fast and sure. The raiders fought back, even as many fell wildly from the saddle. One of them was Walker.

The thunder of guns was so loud that Ben could hardly hear Shockley yelling.

'Stop!' the rancher shouted. 'He got my son!'

The riders fell back. The gunfire gradually halted. The echo of the blasts was as loud as the battle. Soon, there was a deathly silence.

Dead men were all over the ground. Loose horses ran about. Seven raiders were still mounted, sitting with weapons ready, waiting. But they had lost heart. Several wounded attackers were struggling to their feet and recovering their horses. They had no fight left.

Zevala was not among them, but Walker lay dead.

Ben and Clay aimed their arsenal at the survivors. Shockley, wounded in the shoulder, half crawled to his son. Frantically, he cradled Rich in his arms.

'Rich!' he cried, shaking him.

But the young man lay dead in his embrace. The rancher shook him, again and again. No life returned.

Shockley staggered to his feet and glared at Ben and Clay with crazed hate. He shook his fist. 'You're both dead!' he roared.

His warning echoed. His fury was even louder.

The door of the smoke-filled bunkhouse was thrust open.

Barker came out, coughing, rifle in hand. He seemed dazed for a while. Then he glared at Lane Shockley.

'You and your men take your dead and get off my range,' he growled, wiping his eyes with a hand.

The bunkhouse smoldered behind him, but the sod roof had never really erupted in flames. Barker had probably doused it from inside, and it was intact.

Shockley nodded to his men, and then walked over to Barker. His face was red with anger. Blood ran from his shoulder. But he didn't care. The two old men faced each other, a mere five feet apart.

'You ain't seen the last of me, Barker.'

'I'll shoot the first steer that tries to cross.'

'When you're short your fancy guns, I'll be back.'

Ben and Clay stood fast while the men tied the bodies onto the saddles. Shockley took personal care of his son. Soon the scraggly group were making their way toward the river. They disappeared over the far knoll.

Dead men still lay around the sheds and corrals. It was the bloodiest battle that Ben had ever seen, and it sickened him.

'What about your wife and daughter?' he asked Barker.

'I sent them and Carson to the line shack right after you left,' the old man said. 'And you were right about your brother.'

Ben turned to see Jess coming from the smithy.

'As soon as they hit,' Barker said, 'he dived into the shack with Gridley. He musta got half a dozen right off.'

The brothers dismounted. Jess came hurrying over, shaking their hands, hugging Ben, trying to resist doing the same with Clay until Clay explained that the Barkers knew who he was. It was Texas and family all over again. But the smell of death was in the air.

Barker looked at the men lying in the dirt. He shook his head as he spoke. 'Good men,' he said.

Gridley and two other men came out of the smithy. Gridley was limping, with blood on his right leg. Bleeding from the left shoulder, Peters was also limping. The third man, one of the tougher old men, had his head wrapped with a bandanna, but was still bleeding from above his ear.

It had been a terrible loss. Only the brothers hadn't been hit. It was worse than the war. Ben thought of the battlefields with layers of men, but they had been strangers. He had eaten with these men, laughed with them. It hurt to look at them now.

'Range wars ain't usually like this,' Clay said. 'Seems like they were mighty sure of themselves, comin' in without cover.'

'They came chargin' in like Comanches,' Barker agreed. 'Ran right over us.'

Gridley shook his head. 'Too bad Zevala wasn't among 'em.'

'This isn't his style,' Ben said.

'He likes to put on a show,' Clay added.

'They're beat for now,' Barker said, 'but we got to get Zevala. That will take the heart out of 'em.'

Barker had a crease on the side of his forehead. After tying a bandanna around his head, he looked at the smoldering bunkhouse. He could barely stand.

The sound of a horse nickering turned their heads to the north. A sorrel was coming over the hill, led by a limping old man. A woman was astride, slumped over the pommel, skirts draped in all directions. It was Carson and Mrs. Barker.

As they approached, the men hurried as best they could to meet them. Carson was bleeding at the mouth

222

and breathing heavily. His right leg was all wrapped in petticoats, with blood showing through. His face had been badly beaten, and he looked dazed.

Despite his head wound, Barker was able to reach up and help his wife slip to the ground. She lay against his knee as he knelt, holding her against him. Her face was bruised. Blood trickled from her gray hair.

'That Saul Holder,' she moaned, 'he came for Elena. Left us for dead.'

Barker's fury was red fire in his face.

'Don't worry,' Ben said. 'Clay and I will get 'em. Jess, you take care of things here.'

'If he gets up in that forest,' Barker said, 'you'll never find 'em.'

'Don't worry,' Ben said. 'Clay'll track 'em.'

Clay lifted Mrs. Barker in his big arms and carried her to the bunkhouse. Her husband followed anxiously.

'She'll be all right,' Clay assured him.

While Clay was checking Mrs. Barker to make sure that nothing was broken, Ben set about packing their mounts with grub and double bedrolls. He stocked up on shells, checked the Winchester rifles, and placed them in the scabbards.

Soon Clay came outside, followed by Barker. Jess stood aside as his brothers mounted.

Barker came over to Ben's side, and looking up anxiously, he put his hand on the pommel of Ben's Texas saddle. The old man was trembling.

'Ben, I'm beggin' you. Bring her back alive.'

The agony in the rancher's eyes tore at Ben's heart. He nodded, then swallowed hard. He, too, was thinking of Saul's grubby hands. He prayed that Elena would survive.

Ben and Clay turned their horses and rode north. Clay's black kept pace with the big bay.

Already late morning, it would take two hours to the foot of the rim. Ben hoped that Holder knew about the secret trail, perhaps by having followed his tracks when he had rescued Elena the first time. That would make it easier to head in the right direction.

'Getting cloudy,' Clay said.

Ben thought of how Sid had merely tied her up when he was courting her. He feared that this time it would be different. Saul had lost a father and brother, and he had been insulted by the Barkers' disdain for Holder courtship.

Ben bit his lip as he thought of Elena's striking beauty. He had admired her strength and courage. He prayed that they would not fail her now.

At the line shack, Clay stopped and dismounted. Kneeling in the thick grass, he checked the prints. He found signs of a chipped shoe worn by one of the horses.

Clay remounted and they headed full gallop for the rim, resting only when he got down to check the trail. The sun was high in the blue sky, but clouds were moving swiftly from the north. Clay tracked the chipped shoe right through the tracks of the cattle.

Soon they were near the secret deer path that Elena had found. Clay leaned over from the saddle.

'Same print,' he said.

The sky was darkening. Before long, it would rain. Yet Ben was confident that if anyone could track Saul and Elena, it would be Clay.

Their horses fought their way up the steep trail, and they were sweating and panting when they finally reached the top. It was early afternoon. There was no sunlight. The sky was covered with swift black clouds. Lightning flashed across the heavens. There was a rumble far away. It was too warm for snow. It would be rain.

'It's going to wash out everything,' Clay said.

The trail led along the rim, westward over the rocks. Clay managed to find where the horseshoes had creased the stone in two places. Ben pointed out to Clay where he had found Jenson.

Onward they rode, carefully now, conscious of the horses' loud noise on the rocks. Then, abruptly, the trail turned into the thick forest. In one spot, the riders had circled the snow patches in an attempt to hide their sign.

'He's heading for high country,' Clay said.

'We got to let him know we're coming.'

'He's hardly an hour ahead, if that. It'll mean ambush.'

'But it'll stop him from harming Elena.'

Ben's face was hot. He was damp all over under his leather coat. The thought of Saul's just touching that pretty face made him furious.

He drew his Winchester and fired a shot. It echoed for anyone to hear in the forest.

They kept riding. Every half hour, Ben would fire his rifle into the cloudy sky. At midafternoon, they came out of the forest onto a grassy plateau that spread half a mile square before it was lost into another forest.

Reining up, they surveyed the situation.

'If he heard the shot, he could be right over yonder,' Clay said.

'Let's spread out.'

'And ride hard.'

When they had spread about thirty feet apart at the edge of the forest, they turned and looked at each other. One of them could be shot down in the next few minutes.

11

Suddenly, Clay and Ben let out a rebel yell and rode at full gallop across the clearing. Each had a six-gun drawn. Each rode low in the saddle.

Before they reached the other side, a rifle exploded gunfire from the forest, and a bullet whistled past Ben's neck.

The brothers kept riding. Gunfire scattered around them. Clay's horse was hit in the chest. It went sprawling, taking Clay with it.

Ben rode right for the source of the shot. A bullet went through his coat sleeve. Another screamed past his ear. He charged into the forest, right on top of Saul.

The man was desperately trying to work the lever on his Winchester, but it was jammed. He fell aside as Ben's horse nearly struck him. Saul frantically drew his six-gun.

Ben leaped from the saddle, landing on top of him. He smashed him with his fist as they crashed in the thick underbrush. They rolled, struggling to get a grip on each other. Saul's gun went off twice.

They pounded each other. Ben's fist slammed into the man's gut. They rolled again, sweating, breathing hard.

Saul's dirty, bearded face was next to Ben's. The man's little eyes were blazing hot. Ben shoved his fist at his jaw.

Saul's head snapped back, but, recovering, he tried to get his gun between them. He grunted curses.

When Saul finally maneuvered the weapon between their chests, it was knocked down, and it went off right in his own belly. He gasped, wild-eyed. Ben drew back as the man curled up in agony. Reeling back to sit on his heels, Ben saw the man die.

Then, out of breath, sweating, he staggered to his feet.

'Elena!' he called.

'Over there,' Clay said, stumbling through the brush.

Clay was pointing to a red cape in a far thicket.

Ben prayed that she was all right. He felt the first drops of rain as he hurried through the trees. Lightning was slicing across the black sky. When he reached Elena, he came to a halt and stared. She'd been beaten so badly that he barely recognized her. He knelt, his eyes burning. She looked as if she were already dead. Her clothes were still intact. Saul had had time only to try to beat her into submission. Clay hobbled over to stand at his side.

Ben knelt to feel her heart. It was still beating. Clay checked her for broken bones. Her skin was cold.

Slowly, Ben slid his arms beneath her. It was the second time he had lifted her this way. But this time she might not live.

Clay put his hand on her cold face. 'She's got a bad chill,' he said. 'We have to get her warm. She may be busted up inside. That barber much of a doctor?'

'He helped me.'

His left leg sore from the fall, Clay scouted around until he found the two horses, Saul's black and Elena's sorrel mare. Ben didn't want to tie her in her own saddle. They wrapped her in blankets, then Ben mounted and Clay handed her up to him. She settled in his arms, still unconscious, nearly lifeless. Ben put his arm around her and took up the reins.

Elena's condition would easily prove that whatever had been done was justified. Clay covered Holder with rocks and then mounted the man's horse, leading Elena's.

As he rode, Ben regretted that he could never court Elena, even after he collected his pardon. Yet, despite their differences, he felt as if she belonged in his arms.

It seemed an eternity before they reached the rim. They started down the trail in the heavy rain. Water poured from their backs and mounts. When they reached the valley floor, it was already dark.

As they rode across the grassland, Ben thought of the ranch with four hands, the three Darringers, a furious rancher, and twenty thousand head of cattle. The new men would help, but for now, the ranch was in a lot of trouble.

'You know that Zevala will be waiting in town,' Clay said as they rode closer together.

'I know,' Ben said.

But Ben wasn't worried about Zevala just now. All he could think about was Elena, so quiet in his arms. She should have married one of the Sanchez brothers. She'd be safe in Mexico by now.

The fire in the smithy guided them to the ranch. It was still raining heavily. Lightning streaked across the sky. Thunder rolled again and again. The cattle would be skittish, scattering far and wide.

At the smithy they saw Jess, Gridley, and the three hands, huddled in out of the rain. The fire in the pit was whipping in the wind.

Jess and Gridley came outside to help, slickers over their heads. Gridley threw his cover around Elena. Ben drew it tight around her, but she was already soaked. Gridley handed Clay two slickers as Ben rode toward the light in the bunkhouse. Clay rode after him, then dismounted and knocked on the door.

Barker flung it open. His wife was right behind him, her face black and blue. Her hand flew to her mouth when she saw Elena in Ben's arms.

'Is she alive?' Barker asked, pulling on his slicker.

'Barely,' Clay said. 'We got to get her to the doctor.'

'He ain't much of one,' Barker said, 'but he's all we've got. I'll get the wagon.'

Mrs. Barker came out into the rain and reached up to touch Elena's limp hand. Tears filled her eyes and washed down her face. She retreated, then returned with a slicker over her head and shoulders.

Barker and Jess brought the wagon forward. The team was restless in the rain. Elena was lowered into the wagon bed. Mrs. Barker held a slicker over them both.

Barker and Jess climbed onto the wagon seat and set off. Clay and Ben rode on either side. They were all wearing slickers now. When they reached the river, it was rising and roaring like an animal toward the east and the Colorado.

It was so dark that they could barely see their way. The wagon hit the water hard. Ben and Clay each had a rope on the wagon bed, and pulling from both sides, they fought their way across.

At last, they struggled up the other bank and headed east along the river. The rain pounded them. Lightning streaked across the sky.

It seemed forever before they saw the

dim outline of the town. When they reached the barber's, Ben dismounted and banged on the door. At long last it opened. The sleepy little barber rubbed his eyes and let them inside.

Elena was taken to his 'hospital,' a back room with a table stained with blood. The barber spread a sheet across it, and Elena was stretched out, her wet hair spilling down the side. The lamplight was eerie. Rain pounded the roof.

While Mrs. Barker stayed with the doctor and Elena, the three men went back into the barber shop. They sat around, feeling helpless.

'Never had any trouble with that girl,' Barker muttered. 'Just had to keep the men away from her, that's all. Should have left her at that finishing school another year. But she got to grievin' for home.'

A half hour passed. Mrs. Barker came out, looking relieved. 'She'll be all right,' she said, sliding into her husband's arms. 'He's got her awake with smelling salts. We rubbed her down so she got warmer. We can take her with us.'

'We'll all stay at the hotel,' Barker said, tears in his eyes. 'You boys take a room, on me. Nothing we can do at the ranch till the rain lets up.'

The doctor-barber came out, wiping his hands.

'Nothin's broken,' he reported. 'He beat her pretty bad, so she'll be sore for a long time.'

'Maybe you'd best carry her, Ben,' Barker said.

Following Barker into the room, Ben saw Elena sitting up and holding her head in her hands. When she heard them, she slowly looked up. Her face was dark with bruises. She was wrapped in several blankets. She looked dazed.

She saw Ben and lifted a trembling hand.

Swallowing hard, he looked at her father, who nodded. Taking a deep breath, Ben walked over to her. His right hand slid behind her back, his left under her knees. She placed her left arm around his neck as he lifted her. She winced in pain.

Her face rested against his chest, and her hair flowed down to his chest. She felt lighter than ever, like a wisp of a child.

He walked to the front door, where he paused as Barker put a slicker over them. Outside in the rain, she held tight as Ben carried her to the hotel. Up on the porch, out of the rain, he waited for the others to join him.

Inside, the dozing clerk was rudely awakened by the rancher, who signed up for two rooms, one for his family and one for the three men. Ben carried Elena up the stairs. All the while, she clung to him. As he took one step at a time, he suddenly remembered when he had looked at the landing to see Caroline. Caroline, without a fiancé now. Caroline, who still loved him. He was mighty confused.

On the landing, Ben paused while the rancher looked at the room numbers.

Finally, down a hallway, Barker opened the right door. Inside, he turned up a lamp while Ben brought in Elena and slowly laid her on one of the two large beds.

Standing back, Ben looked down at her. She was as lovely as ever. She looked up at him with a gentle smile. Then she closed her eyes.

'Keep her awake for a while,' Clay said. 'And leave the blankets around her until she feels warm again.'

Accordingly, Mrs. Barker hurried to shake Elena and force her to sit up. The three brothers backed out of the room.

Ben looked at the closed door for a while. Then he walked with his brothers down to their own room.

It was also a fine room, with lush furnishings and good beds. They tossed a coin. Ben won and got a bed to himself. Clay and Jess had to share.

'And Clay snores like a donkey,' Jess complained.

Next, they hugged one another and

laughed at their grand reunion. They felt as if they were back in Texas, except that their mother wasn't around to scold them for being so noisy.

Jess sighed. 'All we need now is to find Hank.'

'Soon as Ben gets his pardon,' Clay said.

'If I get by Zevala,' Ben reminded them.

There was a knock at the door and Ben opened it.

Barker looked drawn and weary as he entered and leaned against the door.

'Ben, we was talkin',' the rancher said. 'You've earned that pardon. We'll have a letter for you tomorrow. You can take it to the governor yourself. Shockley and the others are beat down pretty bad. We got time to rebuild. By then, the land grant will be approved.'

'What are you trying to say?' Clay asked.

'We want Ben to ride out now,' the rancher said. 'If he waits around, Zevala will show.'

Ben gazed at the old man. He realized that he was being set free. But he shrugged.

'Won't work,' he said. 'Zevala's got my scent. He'd be on my trail. I'd rather face him here.'

'We'll take the letter, anyhow,' Jess told Barker.

The rancher turned to open the door, and then, with his back to them and his voice choked with hidden tears, he said, 'Ben, thank you for saving her again. I got no way to repay you. Ain't nothin' equal to that.'

As Barker closed the door behind him, Ben swallowed hard, trying to stop his own tears.

'I didn't see any hate in that old man,' Clay said.

The brothers pulled off their boots. Ben dug into one of the saddlebags that Jess had brought along, and they helped themselves to the biscuits and jerky. They sat around talking until late in the night.

★ ★ ★

Ben slept mighty well for the first time in a year. When he awakened the next morning, he sat up and grinned at the sight of his brothers. They were sprawled every which way over the other bed, with blankets twisted and pulled in all directions.

He stretched and stood up, then walked to the window and pulled back the curtains. The sun was shining. It was a glorious day.

There was a knock. A young man said to Ben as he opened the door, 'Mr. Barker says you men are invited to breakfast about now.'

Ben awakened his cranky brothers. They washed up, combed their hair, and pulled on their boots. Downstairs, as they entered the lobby and headed toward the restaurant, Ben paused. Caroline was alone in the room, sitting on one of the couches. Wearing yellow, not black, she looked especially pretty. Her golden curls were set with white ribbons. There was no sign of mourning.

Startled to see him, she stood up. Ben waved his brothers on and walked over to her. She slipped her hands into his.

'Oh, Ben, so much has happened.'

'I'm sorry about Rich Shockley.'

'He was good to me. My family liked him because he had a great deal of wealth and position.'

'Of which I have none.'

'But you had potential, Ben. And you still do.'

'That's up to the Barkers. I either get a pardon or I go back to Yuma.'

'It's all so uncertain,' she said, looking strained.

'What will you do now?'

'What do you think I should do, Ben?'

'Go home to your family.'

'What about *us?*' she asked, moving closer. 'You still love me. I know you do.'

He gazed down at her, wondering

just how true that was. He thought of the letter she had written. He wondered how she would react the next time he was in trouble.

'Ben, you could go back to Texas. When you're a lawyer, we could start over. My family might feel different then.'

'I thought I'd head for California.'

'What do you mean?'

'I could get a job as a lawman, or hire out again.'

Her face turned red. She shook her head. Backing away, she stared at him as she freed her hands.

'Ben, I love you, but I could never live that way.'

He felt guilty for having tested her. He wanted to tell her the truth, that he had high hopes for the pardon, that he wanted to go back to Texas to finish his law studies. There had been a time when he was desperate to provide the way of life she wanted, the money for her fine clothes and trips to the big cities, for a fine house with servants. But everything was suddenly clear. Her love was weak, dependent on his success and on her parents' approval. She just didn't love him enough to overcome her more urgent needs.

His bitterness had been wasted on a woman who couldn't be other than the way she was. Yet, she had always been soft, feminine, and desirable. He was saddened.

They gazed at each other, knowing that this was the last time they would ever see each other. She would go home to her snobbish family with a lot of stories to tell.

Then she nodded at her luggage by the hotel entrance.

'The stage will be leaving soon,' she said. 'I'm sorry, Ben. I'm just not strong enough. I never was. I can tell you now, it wasn't just my uncle that kept me from writing to you. I just didn't have the courage.'

It was a painful speech, but it rang true. He knew now that he couldn't blame her for deserting him. She just wasn't able to do anything else. Now that she was free to follow her heart, she had to admit, even to herself, that she couldn't cross over to his side.

At the hotel entrance, a porter appeared and he carried away her luggage. A couple came from the dining room, carrying carpetbags. Caroline's chaperone also appeared, and she walked ahead to wait outside.

'All aboard,' a bearded man called from the front door.

Caroline watched the others head for the porch. She turned and looked up at Ben. There were tears in her eyes. She reached up and kissed his cheek. He didn't move. She turned and hurried away.

He watched her go, sorry but relieved. Then he turned around and walked to the dining room, where the Barkers were waiting with his brothers.

At a long table near the right wall, the Barkers were seated with Clay and

Jess. The men had removed their hats. Ben carried his in his hand.

As he approached, he saw Elena sitting between her parents, their backs to the wall. She wore a blue cape, and her hair was tied back from her throat. Dark bruises colored her face. She looked at him and smiled. It was a lovely smile. But it was only gratitude, he thought.

He sat between his brothers, facing the Barkers.

'Ben,' Elena said, extending her hand across the table.

Awkwardly, he took it. Her fingers were soft but cold. She withdrew her hand. He glanced at her parents, expecting to see disapproval. But they were looking at their daughter, not at him.

'Elena slept well,' her mother said, and then fussed with Elena's hair.

The waiter came with steaming-hot coffee for everyone. He took their orders and left.

'Clay was telling us about fighting

Apaches down along the Mexican border,' Barker said, amused. 'Some of his stories seem a little stretched out.'

'And Jess,' Mrs. Barker said, 'has promised to get a guitar and sing for us.'

'They're both going to stay and help us with the roundup,' Barker said. 'Seems like the Darringers have been a blessing.'

Elena slowly took out an envelope and handed it across the table to Ben. It was on stationery with the Barker name, and it was addressed to the governor. Ben took it and stared at it.

Elena said, 'I first wrote it after you saved me from Sid Holder. I had to rewrite it after you saved me from Saul. I owe you my life, Ben — four times over.'

'We're very grateful,' her mother said.

Ben couldn't meet their gaze. He was filled to the brim with pleasure. He felt his brothers' warmth. Sipping his coffee, he felt awkward.

'We don't know what happened with our son,' Barker said unexpectedly. 'Maybe we'll never know. But I've been watching you, Ben. I like what I've been seeing.'

'You're a good man, Ben,' Mrs. Barker said.

'We don't want you ridin' on,' the rancher continued. 'I'd be mighty pleased if you'd hire on for good. Same goes for your brothers.'

Ben stared down at the envelope, and then he shook his head. He couldn't say it, but he didn't want to be around when Elena married someone else.

'I'm right sorry, Mr. Barker,' he said. 'I think I'd best be movin' on.'

The sudden silence was so heavy that Ben felt crushed. He couldn't look up. He couldn't move. He knew Elena was watching him. His brothers reached for the food being placed on the table, the golden eggs and savory ham. Ben couldn't smell a thing. All he could do was feel heartache, because he didn't ever want to ride away from Elena.

'Back to Texas?' Mrs. Barker asked.

'My mother wants me to be a lawyer,' Ben said. 'She has this thing about justice.'

'We keep tellin' her she picked the wrong son,' Clay said with a laugh.

'Mr. Barker, Mrs. Barker,' a man's voice said in sudden interruption. 'Nice to see you.' It was the sheriff, standing behind the three brothers.

'Well,' Barker said, 'my daughter's safe, no thanks to you. And if you see Zevala, you tell him to just go home. It's all over.'

'I hope you enjoy your breakfast,' the sheriff said, unfazed. He tipped his hat and smiled, and he was about to walk away when a man called from the doorway:

'Someone in here named Ben Darringer?'

Ben turned to the grizzled stranger. 'That's me.'

'Seems like there's a fella out in the street waitin' for you. Name's Zevala.'

Ben felt cold, clean through.

'He'll have to wait,' Ben said. 'I'm plannin' to finish my breakfast.'

They all glanced at the sheriff, who looked cornered. He made a face as if he had just forgotten something, then headed for the back door of the dining room as fast as he could.

'What you need around here is our brother Hank,' Jess told Barker. 'He's one heck of a lawman. Maybe we could send him along someday.'

'If he fights like the three of you,' Barker said, 'he'd be welcome.'

Silence fell on the table. Everyone had his and her own thoughts. Elena didn't want Ben to suffer harm. Her parents were filled with gratitude and didn't know how to protect him. His brothers wanted to interfere, but they knew that this was something Ben had to handle.

As Ben slowly ate, he hoped that the audacity of his taking time to eat would upset the proud Zevala. More than ever before, he was savoring life, and he didn't want to die. He saw Elena

251

watching him. She looked anxious.

Now that Caroline was gone, he knew why he had been so nervous around Elena. Despite himself, he had fallen in love with her. Not only was she beautiful, she was courageous, gentle, and his dream of the perfect woman.

But her parents would surely say that though he was good enough to save her life, he wasn't fit to marry her.

He finished his coffee, picked up the envelope addressed to the governor, and handed it to Jess for safekeeping.

'Take your time,' Clay suggested. 'It'll make him edgy!'

'Remember,' Jess said, 'he's nobody special. He's just another killer who's been around too long.'

'You don't have to go out there,' Barker told him. 'You got your pardon. You don't owe us nothin'.'

'My husband's right,' Mrs. Barker said.

Ben couldn't explain. All he knew was that he was not going to turn yellow and walk away from Zevala.

He stood up very slowly. His brothers rose with him and followed him to the doorway.

His heart was hammering in his chest. After all this — gaining his freedom, finding Clay, loving a woman he could never have, learning the truth about Caroline — he was going out to face certain death.

'Ben!' Elena cried.

Turning, he was surprised to see her coming around the table. She rushed toward him. Her eyes were wide with fear.

'Oh, Ben,' she said softly.

'Don't worry,' he said.

'Please don't go out there.'

He was overjoyed by her fear for his safety. For a moment, he basked in her concern. As he turned to go, she whispered to him:

'Ben, wait.'

She came closer and offered him her hands. They were cold but soft. The sensation of her touch ran up his arms.

'Ben, I can't let you go out there.'

He looked at her father and mother, who were coming toward them. Barker looked perplexed. His wife looked strained.

'Elena,' Ben said, 'if I don't face Zevala, he'll be after your father next. He won't quit unless Shockley calls him off. And maybe not even then.'

She tried to speak and couldn't. Then she moved forward, threw her arms around his neck, and kissed his lips. He fought the urge to crush her to him. She tasted wonderful. She smelled of roses. She was soft and warm against him.

Her lips clung to his a moment longer. Then, slowly, she stepped away, though Ben would always feel her closeness. There were tears in her eyes, and when a drop trickled down her cheek, he reached up with a finger, touched it, and put it to his lips.

'Stay here,' he said.

Then he walked with his brothers through the lobby and out the door, not knowing if he would ever return.

12

It was midmorning when Ben walked onto the porch of the hotel, his brothers following. The sun was bright but the wind was cool. The stage had already taken Caroline away. There was no one on the street except Zevala.

The killer was standing with his back to the sun, in the middle of the street, down near the livery. The silver conchos on his hat and belt were glittering.

'Are you all right?' Clay asked Ben. 'Do you want me to take him?'

Ben shook his head. His brothers knew that Ben was the fastest among them. If anyone had a chance, it was Ben. Yet they knew that Ben's chance was only fifty-fifty.

'Try to make him nervous,' Jess said.

'You already made him wait till you

finished breakfast,' Clay reminded him. 'Take your time.'

Ben walked to the edge of the porch. His Colts felt heavy at his sides. He could see faces at the windows and behind the swinging doors of the saloon across the street. Zevala had his audience.

Ben stretched and yawned. Lazily, he pulled his hat down low on his brow. Then he walked down the steps onto the muddy ground. His boots squished in the soggy earth as he moved toward the middle of the street. Finally, he turned to look toward the Texas killer, all dressed in black, waiting patiently, or not.

'It is not Sunday,' Zevala said, his accent heavy.

Ben stood with hands dangling near his holsters, the way Zevala was standing. They were some sixty feet apart. They had to be closer. Whoever moved first would be the more fearless.

Slowly, Ben started walking toward

him. Not to be outdone, Zevala also started walking. They were within twenty feet of each other when they both came to a stop.

The sun was not in Ben's eyes because of his hat brim, but it was bright. The stillness surrounding them was stirred only by the wind.

'Call it,' Zevala said.

Ben shook his head. Zevala had to make the first move. It was Ben's way of proving a fair fight. He waited. Zevala just looked at him.

'I heard about your fighting down around Brownsville,' Zevala said. 'And I've seen you draw. I know all about you, Darringer. I am sorry that I am about to kill you.'

Ben didn't move. The gunman was getting edgy. Ben could see it in his flexing fingers, the lowered brows, and tight mouth.

'Someone toss a coin,' Zevala shouted.

A bearded man came out of the saloon. He was flipping a gold piece in his hand. He wanted to be the man who called the fight between Zevala and Ben Darringer.

'Are you ready?' Zevala asked Ben.

Ben nodded, then stood and waited. The coin went spinning into the air. Gleaming in the sun, it reached its apogee where it seemed suspended forever. Then, finally, it fell to earth. As it hit the ground, they both drew at the same time.

Gunfire roared, breaking the stillness. Smoke curled from their guns. Zevala's mouth was twisted into an ugly smile.

Ben felt something hot on his left side, under his arm, but he kept his six-gun level in his right hand, ready to fire again. He felt his strength draining away. Zevala seemed indestructible.

Zevala took a step forward, his weapon aimed. His eyes were narrowed. He was still smiling, though his face was covered with sweat. Suddenly, his gun arm began to waver. Then he paused and leaned sideways.

Ben saw the blood on the man's shirt, just above the heart. Zevala's gun lowered, and then he fell to his knees and stared at Ben. Finally, with a violent shaking, he went face forward into the mud.

There was silence in the street.

When the barber came out of his place of business, he was uncertain if he was to be doctor or undertaker. Kneeling, he turned Zevala and listened to and felt his heart. He finally shook his head. The man was dead.

Onlookers began to appear from doorways.

Ben felt weak. He could barely stand, but his brothers were there to hold him up. Then he realized that he had been hit on his left side. It was painful now, and he felt the blood.

The barber came over to Ben.

'Get him into my place,' he said.

Suddenly, Elena was there, her pretty blue dress lifted from the mud, her satin shoes deep in it. She followed as his brothers helped him over to the barber shop. She went inside with them.

As Ben sat on the table while the barber removed his shirt, she wasn't concerned with modesty. Her parents appeared in the doorway behind her. His brothers stood back to watch.

'Well, you're lucky,' the barber said. 'The bullet went clean through again. I can never practice my other skills with you.'

Ben was a little embarrassed, sitting there without his shirt. He was conscious of his bareness and sweat. He felt too exposed.

The barber began to wrap his entire chest, round and round, with a long bandage. Suddenly, Elena interfered.

'Let me help,' she said firmly.

Ben watched as she took over, tying the bandage with her small hands. After a final tug, as she looked up at him, he saw that same shy look again. The girl who had kissed him had once more retreated into modesty.

'You done it, Ben,' Barker said. 'Now Shockley's got to back off.'

Clay shook his head. 'But every

gunhand who wants a name will come looking for the man who took Zevala.'

'Ben, you oughta ride out with us,' Jess advised.

'We need him,' Elena said, looking away.

For a long time, they all stood awkwardly around Ben.

Then, Elena straightened, and with determination bright in her eyes, she turned to her parents and his brothers.

'Please, leave us alone.'

'Elena!' her mother said. 'It's not seemly.'

'Then you'll just have to watch,' Elena said. She put her hand on Ben's bare arm, and then pulled him off the table to stand in front of her.

Ben didn't know what to say or do.

'Ben,' Elena said, 'you are not leaving without me, so make up your mind. Do you want to stay here and be part of the Barker family, or do you want to go riding off?'

Ben swallowed hard, staring into her deep blue eyes.

'Your parents got a say in this,' he mumbled.

Elena slid her hands up around his neck. She pulled him closer. Her parents were silent, watching. Ben felt hot all over. He fought to keep his hands at his side as Elena stood on tiptoe.

Once again, she kissed him. She tasted delicious. He felt tremors down his body and into his boots.

He could stand it no more. He wrapped his arms around her and hugged her close as he kissed her back. It was a long, sweet embrace. His heart swelled with unbearable joy.

Then Elena drew back in his arms, a lovely smile on her bruised face.

'Ask them,' she insisted.

Ben turned to the Barkers. Mrs. Barker was hesitant but smiling. Barker nodded.

'We saw it coming,' the rancher said. 'We talked about it, and we figured we was stuck with you. So you got our blessings.'

'We'll build two houses,' Mrs. Barker said. 'Maybe you'd like one with a view of the river.'

'Reckon we'll stay around and help,' Clay said, grinning. Jess nodded agreement.

Elena slid from Ben's arms and kissed her parents. Then she kissed Ben's brothers on the cheek. Jess blushed. Clay looked embarrassed. She was radiant.

Returning to Ben, she took his arm and smiled at him.

He wanted to bask in that smile forever.

THE END

**Other titles in the
Linford Western Library**

THE CROOKED SHERIFF
John Dyson

Black Pete Bowen quit Texas with a burning hatred of men who try to take the law into their own hands. But he discovers that things aren't much different in the silver mountains of Arizona.

THEY'LL HANG BILLY FOR SURE:
Larry & Stretch
Marshall Grover

Billy Reese, the West's most notorious desperado, was to stand trial. From all compass points came the curious and the greedy, the riff-raff of the frontier. Suddenly, a crazed killer was on the loose — but the Texas Trouble-Shooters were there, girding their loins for action.